Einstein's
Underpants

Also by Anthony McGowan

For younger readers:

The Bare Bum Gang and the Holy Grail
The Bare Bum Gang and the Valley of Doom
The Bare Bum Gang and the Football Face-off
The Bare Bum Gang Battle the Dogsnatchers

For older readers:

Hellbent
Henry Tumour
(winner of the Booktrust Teenage Prize, 2006)
The Knife That Killed Me

Anthony McGowan

Einstein's Underpants

And How They Saved the World

Corgi Yearling

EINSTEIN'S UNDERPANTS – AND HOW THEY SAVED THE WORLD
A CORGI YEARLING BOOK 978 0 440 86924 5

Published in Great Britain by Corgi Yearling,
an imprint of Random House Children's Books
A Random House Group Company

This edition published 2010

5 7 9 10 8 6 4

The Random House Group Limited supports The Forest Stewardship
Council (FSC®), the leading international forest certification organisation.
Our books carrying the FSC label are printed on FSC® certified paper. FSC is
the only forest certification scheme endorsed by the leading environmental
organisations, including Greenpeace. Our paper procurement policy can be
found at www.randomhouse.co.uk/environment

Set in 15/19.5 pt Bembo Schoolbook by Falcon Oast Graphic Art Ltd.

Corgi Yearling Books are published by Random House Children's Books,
61–63 Uxbridge Road, London W5 5SA

www.**kids**at**randomhouse**.co.uk
www.**randomhouse**.co.uk

Addresses for companies within The Random House Group Limited
can be found at: www.randomhouse.co.uk/offices.htm

THE RANDOM HOUSE GROUP Limited Reg. No. 954009

A CIP catalogue record for this book is available from the British Library.

Printed and bound by CPI Group (UK) Ltd, Croydon, CR0 4YY

For Alex Mohar Csaky

CHAPTER 1

BAD NEWS FOR PLANET EARTH

Admiral Thlugg of the Borgia Empire was in a good mood.

This was unusual.

Admiral Thlugg hadn't been in a good mood for almost eight hundred Earth years — although, in fairness, he was notoriously grumpy, even by Borgia standards.

It was the delicious taste of the three Russian cosmonauts that was responsible. The cosmonauts had been part of the World Space Programme's attempt to explore the moons of Jupiter. Their spacecraft, *Putin's Revenge*, had been picked up by a Borgia scout vessel, which took them back through the wormhole to the main fleet.

Being captured by grumpy aliens is never

very pleasant, but it was most unfortunate that the cosmonauts encountered the Borgia. The Borgia were perhaps the most despicable life form in the galaxy. Their philosophy was simple: they found, they killed, they ate.

Actually, the very term 'life form' didn't really work for the Borgia as they hardly had a form at all, looking as they did like a heavy sneeze come to life. There was no obvious up or down or back or front to them; not even a real inside or out. They had no eyes, ears, mouths or limbs of their own. They did have a sort of internal beak-like tusk, made from a carbon-tungsten alloy, which they used to help break up and digest some of their chewier victims, but that just floated around inside them like a tooth in a jar of marmalade.

However, they did possess the distinctly unpleasant ability to put to temporary use body parts from whatever other species they had just consumed. So Admiral Thlugg had one eye, a hand and a buttock from the cosmonauts protruding from various points around his gelatinous body.

Being eaten by Admiral Thlugg was, of course, very bad news for the cosmonauts.

It was also very bad news for planet Earth.

The Borgia communicated mainly by means of smell, which was, frankly, rather silly (as well as smelly). They had two main venting holes, through which they emitted the complex aromas that constituted their language. Thlugg now vented his commands, wafting out little puffs of yellowy gas into one of the smellocaster tubes that ran around his ship: *Lemon, lavender, kippers, cheese, cheese, hint of mint, mature cheddar, milk left out on a hot day turning but not yet completely sour, cheese.*

Or, in our language: 'Engine room, engage fusion thrusters; helmsman, steer course 4512-987-6049.99; kitchen, put the kettle on.'

The Borgia attack on planet Earth had begun.

★

Very bad news for planet Earth.

But that was not all.

That was not even the worst of it.

Not by a long shot.

Because something else was coming. Something more destructive, even, than the Borgia.

Asteroid c4098 was on its way.

Asteroid c4098 was a hunk of rock the size of Wales, travelling at 127,000 kilometres an hour, approaching from the opposite side of the Earth to the Borgia invasion fleet. In four days' time it was going to crash into the middle of the United States, where it would leave a crater big enough to hold an ocean. In a few moments, every living thing in North America would die, with the possible exception of some especially hardy bacteria.

The matter displaced by the impact would form a mushroom cloud reaching high into the stratosphere. Dust would blow around the world, bringing on a winter that would last for a hundred years.

Never mind global warming, this was global freezing.

And what would be left alive after that time? Those same hardy bacteria. Cockroaches. Rats. Mushrooms.

Bad news, indeed, for planet Earth.

CHAPTER 2
CHECKMATE

Planet Earth was in trouble, but so was the chess club at St Jude's High School. It was in trouble because it had been invaded. Not by Thlugg and his Borgia stormtroopers, but by Big Mac and the other baboons in his gang.

The chess club was made up of every four-eyed brainiac, weakling, dweeb and nerd in the school. Some were gangly beanpoles with the co-ordination of blind baby kangaroos. Some were shaped like cupcakes. Some like teapots. All any of them hoped for was to get through the day without having their dinner money stolen, or their faces rubbed into the dirt, or being chased by a kid with some dog poo on the end of a stick. In short, they were about as cool as a group of fat clowns sipping hot soup in a sauna.

Alexander wasn't as uncool as the other kids in the chess club. In fact he wasn't really uncool at all, apart from being a bit of a maths geek. He had dark-brown hair and a pleasant round face, and would usually smile unless there was a good reason not to. Alexander wasn't even a chess fanatic. He only hung out at the chess club because of his best friend, Mclvyn. Melvyn needed looking after. Melvyn was nice and maybe just a tiny bit boring, but he was also famously unlucky. He was always the one who got poohed on by pigeons or bitten by yappy little dogs or yelled at by mad people in the street.

His worst piece of luck was that on the very first day of school back at the beginning of Year Seven, his mother had dropped him off and given him a sloppy kiss in front of everyone. That kind of thing sticks with you for ever. Since then he'd had to spend most of his break times hiding from the sort of kids who teased you for being kissed by your mum, and by that I mean almost all the kids in the school, and by 'teased' I mean slapped over the head continually until it was time to go home.

So Alexander used to try to keep Melvyn out of harm's way, even if that sometimes meant that Melvyn's bad luck rubbed off on him.

Usually Mr Van was in charge of the chess club, but today he was late. Mr Van was like a grown-up version of the chess-club nerds. He was probably in the staff toilets trying to comb some of the old food out of his beard. The kids in his class would place bets about what you could find in Mr Van's beard. One day it had been some fragments of fried egg. Another time it was several strands of pot noodle. Once it was a whole chip.

Big Mac and his baboons weren't specifically looking for Melvyn when they burst into the chess club, but they were pleased

when they found him there. It was like being
a goldminer, and finding a diamond by
mistake.

'What have we here?' said Big Mac in his
Big Mac voice, which was actually quite
high and squeaky – though it was best not
to mention that or laugh at him for it
or he'd probably kick you in the parts
that would make *your* voice high and
squeaky too.

Melvyn was playing chess with a skinny,
very slightly buck-toothed person called
Felicity, the only girl who went to chess
club.

Melvyn groaned. It was the sort of
timeless sound made all through history by
villagers when they saw the barbarians
ride up on their horses, ready to steal all
their stuff and then burn down their houses
and probably ride away with all the
pretty girls and most of the plain ones as
well, just leaving the cross-eyed and the
chubby behind.

Felicity disappeared. The truth is, she was probably safe.

Melvyn found himself alone in the middle of a circle, with the chess-club brainiacs looking on helplessly, like mice watching a weasel.

'How would you like to *do* this, Wilson?' said Big Mac pleasantly. 'You've got a couple of options. Either you can just hand over your dinner money now, or we can slap your head for a while, make fun of the way your mum kisses you, slap you a bit more, push you around, make you clean the whiteboard with your tongue — the usual things. What do you say?'

Melvyn didn't say anything. He just reached into his blazer pocket and fished around for his two pounds.

'Wait.'

Alexander hadn't meant to say anything either. He knew it was best just to pay up like they always did.

As soon as he said 'Wait,' he knew he was

in trouble. Without realizing how it had happened, he found that he was now in the middle of the circle as well, next to Melvyn. Had he barged through, or had they spread out to engulf him? He wasn't sure.

'It's all right,' said Melvyn, in a mumble. 'I'll just give them the money. It's not worth fighting for it.'

'Very wise,' said Big Mac. He loomed over them like a troll. He had tiny black eyes and a nose like a squashed satsuma.

'No.'

There it was again. The word coming out of Alexander's mouth without him meaning to say anything.

Big Mac swivelled and gave Alexander his black-eyed stare. Alexander felt his knees turn to jelly.

'What?' Big Mac had fat fingers like pink sausages. He was squeezing them into a fist.

'I said no. You can't have his dinner money.'

Big Mac looked surprised for a couple of seconds, and then let out a giggle that would have been cute if it had come from a three-year-old. From a boy the size of a small bus, it was most unsettling.

'What are you, anyway?' he managed to say after he'd got his breath back. 'I don't even know your name. At least everyone knows who Mummy's Boy here is. But you, you're virtually invisible.'

The trouble with Big Mac was that he wasn't as stupid as he looked (or sounded). What he'd said was exactly what Alexander most feared about himself – that he was a nonentity, a nothing. When he'd said 'No' to Big Mac earlier, it had come out of nowhere. It was as if he were a ventriloquist's dummy, speaking someone else's lines. But now a sea of rage and frustration boiled up inside him, and the words that followed were a surfer riding the wave.

'My name's Alexander, and you can't have Melvyn's dinner money and you can't have mine. Now get lost, you squeaky-voiced fat baby, before I throw you out.'

It was the single bravest thing Alexander had ever done. Admittedly, there wasn't much competition. The second bravest thing was probably when he got a splinter and didn't cry too loudly while his mum pried it out with a needle.

If Alexander thought that his brave words would intimidate Big Mac, he was to be disappointed.

'Excellent,' Big Mac said. 'I huven't had an excuse to thump anyone for ages.' He held his sausagey fingers up in front of his face. 'Poor little guys,' he said sweetly. 'Been feeling all left out? I've been neglecting you, haven't I? Well, time to play.'

Then Big Mac pulled back his fist, ready to deliver the sort of thump that would knock out a tractor. Alexander considered ducking, but the trouble is that anyone who has to think about ducking has already been hit.

That Alexander *wasn't* was due to the fact that at that very moment Mr Van arrived, dragged along by Felicity.

'Good to see you here, Donald,' he said loudly. 'Always nice to have new members of the chess club. Why don't you play me, and we can see what sort of standard you are, eh?'

Big Mac's fat fist was stuck in the air, looking faintly ridiculous. He stared at it for a moment, then scratched his head. 'I was just going, sir,' he replied squeakily. 'I'll see you later,' he said menacingly, looking at Alexander.

Then he and his sidekicks sloped off.

'Thanks,' said Melvyn, looking at his friend strangely.

Alexander shook his head and shrugged his shoulders, as if to indicate that he had no explanation for what had just occurred. He spent the rest of the day feeling puzzled and slightly scared. But nothing else unusual happened – on that day, at least.

CHAPTER 3
UNCLE OTTO

Alexander wasn't sure what was going on to begin with. In his dream, the blobby monster that was chasing him suddenly stopped, opened its horrible toothless mouth and started singing the theme from *Neighbours*.

Alexander woke up.

Must change that stupid ring tone, he thought to himself as he answered his mobile.

'Hello?' he said sleepily.

'ALEXANDER, ALEX, LEXIE LEX, EX.'

'What . . . ? Who . . . ? Oh, hello.'

Alexander realized it was his uncle Otto, the mad scientist.

Uncle Otto wasn't really Alexander's

uncle, he wasn't really called Otto, and he wasn't really a scientist, although he was probably mad. Uncle Otto was related to Alexander in some very obscure way that nobody in his family quite understood, involving second cousins, a secret marriage, an adoption, a long prison sentence, a divorce, and a baby found on a doorstep with a note pinned to its blanket saying: *Plese luk aftor me or I'll probibbly dye.*

Uncle Otto was originally called Kevin, and for a long time he worked in a super-market, eventually becoming assistant deputy manager of his local Tesco. He seemed happy enough, walking around the aisles, making sure that there were enough tins of baked beans and dog food, and that they didn't get mixed up, and he became very good at fixing the tills when they jammed, which was once every fifteen minutes.

But about five years before the events related here, he had climbed on top of the milk cabinet and declared to the world that he was no longer an assistant deputy manager of Tesco but a scientist, doing ground-breaking work on the origins of the universe. He added that semi-skimmed milk was Satan's wee-wee and that eating yogurt made you blind.

Strangely, Tesco decided that they didn't particularly want him working for them any more, and from that day on he was free to dedicate himself to scientific research. He changed his name to Otto because, as he put it, 'It's a good name for a scientist.'

Alexander's mum and dad were the only members of the family who stayed in touch with Otto (or Kevin). Once a month they would go round to his small flat and make sure he was OK. Usually, Uncle Otto wasn't OK, at least as far as Alexander's mum and dad were concerned. Sometimes he would have built a sort of den in his living room made of silver-foil takeaway food cartons.

'Their mind rays can't penetrate the foil,' he explained.

Sometimes he would speak his sentences backwards. Or, in his own words, *Backwards sentences his speak would he sometimes*. Because that way, he told Alexander in a confiding tone, 'Saying I'm what understand can't they.'

He never got round to saying exactly who 'they' were – although, as we'll find out, that eventually became quite clear to Alexander.

Whatever the rest of his family thought, Alexander loved his uncle Otto. During their visits he would sit entranced listening to Otto's ideas about the universe. The great scientist had a telescope set up in his loft, looking out through the skylight. He claimed it was the most powerful telescope in private hands, although Alexander was sure he'd seen the same model for sale in Argos for £49.99, including a free book to help you identify the stars. Alexander would look through it into the night sky, but all he could ever see was smudges and splotches, and not the moons, planets, galaxies and alien spacefleets Uncle Otto claimed were there.

Back to that phone call.

Alexander checked his alarm clock. It was 4.30 a.m.

'Do you realize what time—'

'They're coming for me!' Uncle Otto sounded pretty intense.

Alexander had invented his own scale for working out what sort of mood Uncle Otto was going to be in. The mildest, least insane Otto was just 'batty'. From there the scale went through 'fruitcake' to 'bananas', 'loop-the-loop', 'mad as a monkey on a trike', all the way up to 'screaming loony'.

Now, Alexander reckoned that Uncle Otto was about halfway between loop-the-loop and monkey on a trike.

'Who's coming for you?' he asked sleepily.

'Can't explain now. Come round right away.'

'But, Uncle Kevin – I mean, Otto, it's the middle of the night . . .'

'Who cares about the time? Don't you realize the future of the planet is at stake?'

'How? What do you mean?'

'I can't explain over the phone. They monitor all communications. I can't block them.'

'I can't come round now. My mum . . . she'll go crazy.'

Uncle Otto started screaming at the top of his voice: 'BUT THEY'RE COMING. THEY'RE COMING NOW! THEY'RE COMING TO EAT US. IT'S ALL DOWN TO YOU AND ME. WE'RE THE ONLY ONES WHO CAN SAVE HUMANITY!'

'OK, OK. I'll be there in twenty minutes.'

That calmed Uncle Otto down, and he stopped screaming.

Alexander got up and pulled on his jeans and jumper over his pyjamas. He looked out of his window. The first glimmerings of dawn were lighting the edges of the world. A massive yawn bubbled up from somewhere around his knees and burst out of his mouth. *Five minutes*, he thought, *won't make any difference*. He lay back down on his bed and closed his eyes.

When he opened them again, it was half past eight. Nobody had woken him yet because it was Saturday, but he could hear sounds from downstairs — his little brother watching cartoons, his dad burning the toast in the kitchen ('*Aaarghhh!* Blast stupid toaster'), etc. etc. Alexander really wanted to go and watch the cartoons with his brother and eat some toast washed down by a cup of tea with four spoons of sugar in it. But his conscience wouldn't let him. He put on his socks and trainers and slipped quietly out of the back door.

CHAPTER 4

THEY TAKE POOR OTTO AWAY

Driven by guilt, his legs a spinning blur, Alexander cycled the two kilometres to his uncle's flat in five minutes.

He was fast, but he wasn't fast enough.

By the time Alexander reached Uncle Otto's flat above the butcher's shop in the High Street, the crowd had already assembled. Old ladies in vast coats, bald-headed men with sticks, fat mums clutching snotty-nosed toddlers all gathered to watch Uncle Otto being carried out by some burly ambulance men, helped by six police officers. Otto was strapped to a stretcher so he couldn't even move his arms. But they couldn't stop him from screaming.

'*You're all doomed!*' he yelled. 'They're

coming to get you. They'll eat every last one of you. Then you'll be sorry.'

The crowd didn't look very surprised to hear all this from Otto. Most of them had heard him yelling something similar from the window over the butcher's shop for the last couple of years.

Alexander pushed his way to the front of the crowd. Uncle Otto's wild eye swivelled and caught him.

'Alexander, Alex, Lexie Lex, Ex,' he hissed. 'Come here, boy.'

As Alexander approached, one of the policemen put his hand on his chest. 'Close enough, lad,' he said. 'This chap's dangerous. He's been ranting and raving. There've been complaints.'

'He's not dangerous,' said Alexander. 'He's my uncle.'

He jinked past the policeman, wormed his way between two of the astonished medics and reached the stretcher. He clutched Otto's tethered hand.

'Are you OK, Uncle?' he asked with tears in his eyes.

He felt terrible. If only he'd come round when Otto had telephoned. He could have calmed him down, soothed him, got him talking about the planets and space and not this other crazy stuff.

'These madmen don't know what they're doing,' replied Otto, spraying spittle like a garden sprinkler. 'I've got the co-ordinates. I know which way they're coming. I've picked up their transmissions.'

'Please just shush, Uncle,' Alexander said soothingly. 'If you just keep quiet for a while they'll let you go.'

'Not if they're secretly working with the others. Yes, that's it. They've been infiltrated. THEY'RE HERE ALREADY. THEY'RE EVERYWHERE.'

'That's enough, son, I said.' The policeman grabbed Alexander and tried to pull him away. 'You're only getting him worked up.'

But Uncle Otto's claw-like hand gripped Alexander's. 'Alexander, listen. My observatory. My notes. I've left them for you. And instructions. It's down to you now. Trust no one.'

And then he hissed, 'Here, here!'

Alexander bowed his head, and his uncle whispered something in his ear.

And then the stretcher was away, strong arms barging past.

CHAPTER 5
EAT NO YOGURT

Alexander watched as the doors of the ambulance slammed shut. The crowd drifted away, and he was left alone on the street. It was only then that he realized there was something in his hand.

It was a set of keys. The keys to Otto's flat.

There were two keys for two doors. The first was outside, next to the butcher's. As ever, Alexander was captivated for a moment by the grisly pink specimens in the window. Poor Otto was a vegetarian, and it grieved him to have to live over such a place, but the council had put him there.

The next door was at the top of a flight of dingy stairs smelling faintly of meat and blood. Not knowing what he was going to find, his heart racing, Alexander opened the door.

Otto's place was always a bit of a mess, but he'd never seen it like this. There was junk everywhere. Empty bottles, sweet wrappers, scrunched-up tissues. There were half-eaten pizzas crawling like mutant monsters out of boxes. Fat bluebottles buzzed lazily. The place smelled like a vulture's burp. The TV was turned to face the wall, as if Otto was concerned that its screen concealed an ever-watching eye. On a shelf sat at least thirty naked Barbie dolls, their hair in disarray, looking like they'd witnessed some terrible act of barbarity. What were they there for? A warning? A threat? Or were they just Otto's friends, like the panda that Alexander still kept in his bedroom and had to hide whenever his mates came round to play?

But this wasn't what Alexander had come to see. To reach the laboratory and observatory Uncle Otto had constructed in his loft you had to pull down a complicated folding ladder contraption. It had always seemed like an adventure to Alexander, but now his heart was filled with dread. As he climbed, his imagination filled the loft with bizarre monsters, yellow-eyed lizard men, beetles the size of dogs, human kebabs.

He pushed back the trapdoor, stuck his head through the square opening, and felt around for the light switch. Just as he flicked it on, his hand landed on something furry, and he screamed like an eight-year-old girl finding a spider in her curds and whey.

Dead rat?

Severed head?

Coughed-up hairball?

Alexander blinked in the light.

No.

It was just his uncle's purple bobble hat.

He pulled himself up and looked around. The floor was covered with newspapers, most of them elaborately annotated in green marker pen. Sections had been cut out and rearranged. Some pages had been violently slashed, as if with a machete.

Almost every square inch of the walls was covered in scribbles in the same green marker pen. There were numbers and equations and diagrams and, amid much that was utterly incomprehensible, the occasional blunt statement.

THEY ARE COMING
THEY WILL EAT YOU
WE ARE DOOMED
YOGURT WILL MAKE YOU BLIND

The plastic telescope was in its usual place, aiming up through the skylight, and nearby three ancient rubbishy computers stood shoulder to shoulder on a desk made out of an old door propped up on legs made of piles of books. Otto had told Alexander that the computers were networked together, forming the most intelligent supercomputer in the world outside of NASA. He said they were more powerful than the Death Star. Alexander actually reckoned that the real computing power from the three beige boxes was about equal to his digital watch.

He sat in front of one of the computers, moved the cup of cold tea that stood in the way, and hit the keyboard, waking the machine from sleep.

A box appeared, asking for a password. Alexander typed: EATNOYOGURT. It was what Otto had whispered in his ear.

The screen blinked a couple of times, and then Alexander found himself in the middle of an operating system he'd never even seen before. There were no desktop pictures, no icons, nothing but green letters and numbers on a black background, and a blipping cursor.

Eventually he figured out how to do a system-wide search. Not long after he found a file named: FORALEXTOPSECRET.doc.

His heart thumping, his mouth dry, he hit the return key, and the document appeared on the screen.

CHAPTER 6
UNCLE OTTO'S MESSAGE

My dear nephew Alexander,

If you are reading this note it means that something tragic has happened. I have probably been captured by the enemies of humankind. They may well be eating me now, taking great big bites out of my legs, buttocks, nose, etc. etc. If they are not eating me, then they will no doubt be performing hideous experiments on me, the nature of which I cannot even begin to describe as you are only a kid and they will give you nightmares, although they probably involve sticking things into me using all available orifices. By the way, if someone else apart from my nephew Alex is reading this, then GO BOIL YOUR HEAD, YOU EVIL SPY. YOU STINK. AND YOUR MUM

STINKS. AND YOUR DAD IS A TOILET CLEANER.

As you (I mean Alexander, not the evil spy whose dad is a TOILET CLEANER) know, for several years I have been monitoring inter-galactic radio communications. Most of the millions of messages I have picked up were in code, which delayed me for some time. However, I have now cracked the code, using a decoding device of my own devising. The message is clear.

The invasion has begun.

DO NOT DOUBT THIS.

I have confirmed it with astronomical observations, using my own nuclear telescope, and by studying the behaviour of bats, owls, foxes, wolves and other nocturnal species.

The governments of Earth are too dumb to understand the threat they face, and even if they did understand it, they are too stupid to act decisively. Too stupid or, AS I SUSPECT, already INFILTRATED AND PREPARED FOR BETRAYAL. I, and I alone, have foreseen all this. How? you ask. Me, an ordinary scientist? I'll tell you. Many years ago I was given a precious gift at an international conference for cosmologists, which for security reasons took place at an institution for the care of the insane. A renowned German physicist called BARON LUDWIG SZCHITOFF gave me a wondrous garment that had once belonged to the greatest of all scientists, ALBERT EINSTEIN. This garment had MAGICAL PROPERTIES. The very soul of Einstein had been INFUSED INTO THE FABRIC. As a consequence, anyone who wears the garment gains a portion of the great man's intelligence. This will turn them into a GENIUS.

Like many things, this item of clothing could be used either for GOOD or EVIL. In the wrong hands (or legs) it has the destructive potential of a thousand thermonuclear weapons. In the right hands (or legs) it will save the world. Probably. Therefore I have concealed this item in a cunning hiding place that you, and you alone (that's Alexander, not the STINKY SPY – didn't I tell you to get lost?)

– where was I? Oh, yes – that you and only you will know about.

When you have found the sacred garment, you must begin the battle. You can fight alone but, as I have discovered, alone you cannot win. To win you must gather about you a confederation of allies, a league of heroes, a round table of valiant knights.

This is all I have to say. I hear the approach of the ENEMIES OF MANKIND.

Goodbye and good luck.

OttoAAAAAAAAAAAAAAAAAARRRRRGGGGGGGGGGGG HHHHHHHHHH . . .

CHAPTER 7
HOT WATER

Alexander was stunned. What could he do? There was no clue as to the whereabouts of the mysterious garment. And just what was it, anyway? A cardigan? A vest? A hat? On a whim Alexander went and picked up the purple bobble hat and brought it back to the desk. It didn't look like the kind of thing Einstein would have worn.

This is all just stupid, he thought, and sent the hat gyrating away like a woolly flying saucer. Uncle Otto was a certified nutcase. The world wasn't in peril, or at least not in the way he thought it was.

He spun round on the swivel chair, ready to leave the smelly flat for the last time. As he twisted, his elbow caught the edge of the keyboard which, in turn, bashed into the cup of cold tea.

The tea spilled out all over the table.

'Drat,' said Alexander, thinking what a pain it was going to be to clean it up.

Tea.

The thought triggered something. Something about tea. About Uncle Otto and tea.

Or rather, Uncle Otto and his kettle.

Otto was convinced that people were trying to poison the water in his kettle. To thwart them, he had two kettles – the *dummy* kettle he always left on display when he went out, and the *real* one he actually used to boil his water, which he kept hidden.

And Alexander knew where.

He rushed down the ladder and went into the bathroom. He opened the lid of the toilet bowl, and there was the kettle. Feverishly, he opened the kettle. Then his heart sank. Nothing. The kettle was empty, except for the scummy toilet water.

He sat on the loo, disheartened. And

then, *ping!* It came to him. Otto was convinced that They were spying on him. He'd guess that They knew about his ruse with the kettle. So what would he do? He'd only pretend to use the dummy kettle, while secretly using the *real* kettle. The real one was the dummy, and the dummy one was real.

Alexander rushed back to the kitchen, lifted the kettle lid, and there, nestling in the dark heart of it, he found what he was looking for. He picked the thing out. It was a sort of pale grey colour, smudged with darker hues. Alexander guessed it had once been white. He unfolded it gingerly.

Pants.

Underpants.

Y-fronts.

Big.

Alexander dropped them with a squeal. 'Yuck.'

Was this really the wondrous garment Uncle Otto had told him about? Einstein's underpants?

What a nutter.

Alexander thought about simply throwing them away. Or just leaving them where they were on the dirty lino of the kitchen floor. They looked like they'd be able to crawl off on their own to die in the corner. Or perhaps they'd mate with a cockroach and have lots of mutant underpant babies, scuttling about like floppy tortoises.

But he couldn't just walk away from the underpants. What if Otto was right? What if it really was down to him to save the world? And what if the only way he could do that was with the help of the grundies?

Alexander found a plastic bag and scooped up the pants, trying hard not to let them touch his skin. Then he returned to Otto's lab, looked around for a screwdriver, opened the cases of the three old computers and removed the hard drives. And then, with his plastic bag of unwashed pants and crazy data slung over his handlebars, he cycled home.

CHAPTER 8
ALGEBRA

Alexander had been sweating blood over algebra. The thing was, he just didn't get it. He was good at maths. He was very good at maths. Give him numbers and he was happy. Adding, subtracting, multiplying, dividing, percentages — with those he was like a porpoise gambolling in the sea. He loved geometry and trigonometry. He never bothered with a calculator, even when one was allowed — he just found it easier to do it in his head or on paper.

But that all changed when, instead of numbers, letters appeared. He knew his times tables up to 20 x 20, but when he saw even an easy algebra problem — say, if $x = 4$, $y = 6$ and $z = 9$, then solve $(x + y)(y + z)$ —

his brain turned to porridge. Algebra was his kryptonite. He reckoned he must have had some kind of nasty algebra experience when he was a kid. Maybe he'd fallen into a big pot of alphabetti spaghetti or something.

This was bad for Alexander's morale. Being good at maths was important to him, central to the person he was. If he'd been good at loads of other things as well – the shot put, country dancing, basket weaving, whatever – it wouldn't have mattered so much. But being good at maths was pretty well it, for Alexander. And that was partly why he'd disguised his algebraphobia. Hidden it. Lived a lie. If anyone found out that he couldn't do simple algebra, then a big part of his personality would be exposed as a sham. He'd lose the respect of his fellow nerds, and that would be the end of him.

Up till now it had worked fine. They hadn't really done any algebra in Year Seven. But now it had arrived. In class he'd hit on a brilliant ruse. When Mr McHale asked for the answer to the problem he'd written on the board, Alexander shot his hand up, knowing that the teacher would say, 'OK, Alexander, let's give someone else a chance for a change.'

But there was no escaping this first algebra homework assignment. Asking his mum and dad for help was pointless. May as well ask Umberto, their goldfish. Mum would say, 'Ask your father,' and his dad would say of course he'd help, then sit next to him huffing and puffing and becoming increasingly frustrated, and then getting in a wild temper with the book — throwing it in the corner and saying it must have been printed wrong or something — and then going back to reading the newspaper.

It was then that Alexander thought of the underpants. They were still in the plastic bag under his bed. He'd hidden them there because he wasn't quite sure how he could explain having an old man's underpants without making him and Otto sound like total psychos.

But now he was desperate.

He reached under the bed and got out the pants. He held them up to the light. They had obviously been laundered. But that didn't mean they were nice and clean. There was a mottled pattern of stains and blotches so ingrained that they were now just part of the pants, the way the brown liver-spots on his granny's hands were part of her.

No way was he going to put these on under his trousers. That was icky beyond endurance.

He tried pulling them on over his trousers. There was plenty of room for that. Einstein, Alexander concluded, was a bit of a porker. He looked at himself in the mirror. He'd never felt so stupid in his life. He looked like . . . Well, there was nothing really that he looked like except for a kid wearing a pair of old man's underpants over his trousers.

He sat at his desk and, still not quite believing what he was doing, opened his books.

The first question was:

$$10x - 2 = 7x + 4$$
Find the value of x.

He stared at it.

It stared back at him.

They were like two animals meeting in the jungle at night, not quite sure what to make of each other.

Alexander waited for the pants to kick in, to send their signal to his brain.

Nothing.

He felt like an idiot for even thinking that the pants might help him with his homework. He pulled them off and threw them in the corner. Tomorrow he'd burn them with the leaves in the garden. Except they would probably give off toxic smoke and gas everyone in the street, and the police would come and arrest him, and at his trial it would be revealed that not only was he rubbish at algebra but he'd also put on a pair of dead man's underpants. Live that one down at school he certainly wouldn't.

Then Alexander had another thought. Probably a mad one. The underpants, when worn in the conventional area – i.e. covering your bum – were a very long way from the area you used for solving algebra problems – i.e. your brain. Perhaps if they were closer . . .

Worth a shot, now he'd travelled this far on the road to insanity.

He retrieved the pants and, feeling a torrent of emotions, including shame, excitement, humiliation, shame, shame, embarrassment and shame, he put the pants on his head.

He looked at himself in the mirror again. He looked like a kid with a pair of old underpants on his head. He started to laugh.

He laughed so much that he slumped onto the floor.

It was while he was on the floor that something else happened to Alexander. His mind started to whirr. It was most peculiar. Something, he thought at the time, to do with the laughter bringing oxygen to his brain.

He stopped laughing and stood up.

'Why not have another look at that problem?' he said aloud to himself.

He stared again at the numbers and letters. Then he picked up his pencil and began to write.

$$10x - 2 = 7x + 4$$
$$10x - 2 + 2 = 7x + 4 + 2$$
$$10x = 7x + 6$$
$$10x - 7x = 7x + 6 - 7x$$
$$3x = 6$$
$$x = 2$$

It was easy. Why hadn't he seen it before? He raced through the other nine problems

in five minutes flat. He felt exultant. He felt
. . . extraordinary. He'd cracked algebra. He
was . . . he was . . . a genius.

There was a knock at his door, and his
mother said, 'Alexander?'

'Come—' he began, and in the nick of
time remembered to rip the pants off his
head.

CHAPTER 9
CONTACT

His mother came into the room carrying the cordless phone. She had the sort of neutral expression on her face that Alexander had learned to fear.

'It's for you,' she said.

He hadn't even heard it ring, he'd been so wrapped up in his algebra.

'Who . . . ?'

'Uncle Kevin.'

Otto!

His mother waited for a couple of seconds, and then Alexander closed the door gently in her face. He wasn't a slamming-the-door kind of kid.

'Hello,' he said.

He was expecting the usual flood of

words from Otto. All he got was a subdued, 'Hi.'

Then a pause.

'Everything OK, Otto?'

Another pause. Alexander thought he heard the sound of footsteps echoing down the phone line.

'I'm on the pay phone in the corridor. It's hard to speak. They listen.'

'You sound funny, Uncle.'

'They've been giving me drugs. I fight them, but they are too strong.'

'I'll come and see you soon.'

'No! You must not. Did you find the . . . *you know what.*'

'The pants?'

'Shhhh!'

'Er, yes.'

'Have you tried them?'

'Well, actually I just did.'

'And?'

'I think they, er, that is to say, well, I think they did something. They made me *see . . .*'

Otto sighed contentedly. 'Yes, yes. Now you understand. And once you have understood, then it's time to act.'

For a second Alexander thought that Otto was talking about his homework. 'Yeah, I'll hand it in tomorrow—'

'What are you jabbering about, boy? Don't you comprehend the seriousness of this? Now I have been incarcerated, you are the Earth's only hope.'

The drugs had definitely dulled Otto's frenzy, but his intensity still burned like phosphorus. And even though Alexander knew that his uncle had serious mental problems, he found it almost impossible to resist his will.

'But what can I do? I'm only a kid.'

'You read my message?'

'Yes, but—'

'Then you know your mission. You must form a league of heroes. When the attack comes, you will be the resistance. You will be an underground army. And, guided by the *you know whats*, you will know where and how to strike.'

'But where will I find superheroes around here? It's not exactly Gotham City, is it?'

'Seek and you shall find.'

'And what shall I tell them? I'll need some kind of proof . . . I mean, no one's going to believe any of this.'

'You have my data?'

'I think so – I took the hard drives out of your—'

'It's all there. But remember, time is running out. Act now or it's the end of humanity. I can't talk any more.'

'Are they listening again?'

'No, my money's run—'

And then Otto was cut off.

It took Alexander a long time to get to sleep that night. His mind churned and toiled. He lay under his duvet, writhing with embarrassment at the very idea of recruiting superheroes to fight some kind of alien invasion. He knew that the sane thing would be to simply ignore Uncle Otto. But two thoughts nagged and chewed at his brain, like dogs at a bone. What if he was right? What if something really terrible was going to happen to the world, and he was the only one who could save it? And then there was the ludicrous fact that the pants, Einstein's underpants, had really seemed to give him the power to do his algebra homework.

It was no good. He got up, attached the hard drives to his laptop, and, after he'd put Einstein's underpants on his head, delved into the data.

When he finally drifted to sleep some hours later, he dreamed of monsters again.

And Admiral Thlugg? He too was dreaming, lying upon his soft and swampy bed in his private quarters.

And when a Borgia dreams, he dreams of killing.

Killing slowly.

Killing deliciously.

Drawing out the juice, that delicious liquid centre that all living things possessed.

When he woke up ready for duty, he found that he had eaten his pillow.

CHAPTER 10
THE BIRTH OF UNLUCKEON

'You *are* kidding?' exclaimed Melvyn.

Before Alexander had the opportunity to stress that no, he wasn't kidding, and yes, he was deadly serious about the need to form a league of superheroes to defeat the forces that were massing to conquer the Earth and eat all its inhabitants, human, animal, vegetable and quite possibly mineral as well, Melvyn managed to walk into a wall, bounce backwards, trip over a passing black cat and land on his backside in the middle of the only puddle on an otherwise utterly bone-dry pavement.

Alexander and Melvyn had been walking to school together, as they did most days.

Alexander helped Melvyn back to his feet.

'I'm going to have a wet bum all morning,' Melvyn said in a matter-of-fact way. He'd grown used to this sort of thing and it didn't bother him much any more. 'I expect everyone will think I've had an accident in my trousers.'

Alexander nodded. It *was* what people would think. The best Melvyn could hope for was that everyone would assume he'd simply wet himself rather than having had some sort of titanic diarrhoea episode in his pants. But, knowing Melvyn's luck, some other kid in the classroom would let fly with a super stinky fart at exactly the moment everyone noticed the huge stain on his trousers, and two plus two would be put together and inexorably equal the fact that Melvyn had poohed himself.

'I know it sounds crazy,' Alexander said, shaking the thoughts of what might or might not happen to Melvyn from his head, 'but I think that this time Uncle Otto was on to something.'

'Your uncle Otto is a fruitcake. You told me he believed that he was being followed by specially trained badger assassins.'

'OK, so the badgers were a bit silly. And even Otto admitted in the end that it wasn't a disguised badger but an old bucket, and it wasn't following him but just lying there. And I'm not saying he's the most sane person in the universe, but that doesn't mean he's always wrong. Even a broken watch is right twice a day.'

Melvyn just shook his head.

'Think about it,' Alexander continued. 'What if this is one of those times – the times when the broken watch happens to be right? What if the world really *is* doomed, and we had the chance to do something about it, and we blew it, just because . . . just because . . .'

'Just because it all sounds completely mental?'

'Exactly. But the thing is, it *isn't* completely mental.'

'It must be contagious. Or hereditary. Or both.'

'No, listen to me. You know those drives I took out of Otto's steam-powered computers?'

'Don't tell me you found something on there, did you? Nothing, you know, creepy . . .'

'No, nothing like that. Numbers.'

'Numbers? Was he playing the lottery or something?'

'Maybe, sort of. It was the stuff he said he'd picked up from his aerials. All in binary. Ones and noughts. Hundreds of millions of ones and noughts. To begin with it looked like white noise, just meaningless numerical static. But he said he'd seen patterns in there, so I ran it through a couple of mathematical programs I downloaded. Let them do the number-crunching for me. First they converted the binary into normal numbers, and then . . .'

Melvyn looked interested, or at least not completely bored. 'And then what?'

'And then, well, I don't know exactly.

Even understanding how these programs work is beyond me. But the thing is, they found patterns. They really did. The numbers weren't meaningless.'

'So what did they mean?'

'Search me. All I can say is that this stuff wasn't random. It was produced by some kind of intelligence. And it didn't come from Earth.'

'You're sure?'

'Nope. I'm not sure about anything. But that's what it looks like to me. And that's why we have to do something.'

'Shouldn't we tell the authorities? NASA or the government or, I don't know, someone like that?'

'What, write them an email saying that my insane uncle, who hid Einstein's underpants in his dummy kettle, thinks we're about to be invaded by aliens? That'll go straight to the prime minister with URGENT stamped on the file, won't it?'

'He did *what* with Einstein's underpants?'

'Ah, did I not mention them yet? Well, you see, someone gave Albert Einstein's pants to Otto, and Einstein's genius has somehow been imprinted on them—'

'Like a skid mark?'

'Yes, exactly! The skid mark of genius! And that genius gets passed on to whoever wears the pants. Because in a way that's what genius is − I mean, a thing from within you that leaves its mark, or stain, on the world.'

'Please don't tell me you believe this.'

'I do believe it. I mean, I don't believe it. I mean, I sometimes do and sometimes don't.'

They walked in meditative silence for a while, during which time Melvyn got pooed on by a pigeon and stumbled over an almost imperceptible irregularity in the pavement. Then he said, 'Have you actually tried them on?'

Alexander nodded sheepishly.

'And?'

'And what?'

'Did you turn into a genius?'

'I'm not sure. It's hard to tell. How would you know?'

'Did you have any super-amazing thoughts? Did you solve Gödel's last theorem? Did you have a great idea for ending world hunger?'

'Not as such, no. But geniuses don't have great thoughts all the time, do they? They must have some periods when they're just idling along, thinking about what's on the telly that night and having a cup of tea.'

'So, no effect at all then?'

'I didn't say that.' Alexander was reluctant to tell even his best friend that he'd needed Einstein's help with his algebra.

'Look, I did an experiment. There were some tricky problems, and I couldn't work them out, but when I put on the underpants . . . well, I sort of could. It was amazing, really.'

Melvyn sighed. 'OK then, let's assume that you're right, and that the world is about to be invaded, and that Einstein's underpants have turned you into a genius. What do you want us to do next?'

'Otto said we can't do it on our own. We have to find the other superheroes.'

'What do you mean the *other* super-heroes?'

'I mean the others as well as us.'

'Us? Since when were we superheroes?'

'You admitted that I've got super-intelligence when I wear Einstein's under-pants, yeah?'

'Yeah,' said Melvyn sceptically.

'So that's me sorted. And you – well, you do have a sort of special power.'

'Do I?'

At that moment a bus (the number thir-teen, of course) rumbled past them on the High Street. One of its fat tyres rolled over the corpse of a mouldy, blackened banana. The laws of physics, biology and chemistry should have dictated that the banana was simply squished beneath the tyre, but the laws of the natural universe would often behave erratically around Melvyn, and now they conspired to send the pulpy mass of rank banana matter shooting towards him like a huge gobbet of phlegm fired from a giant footballer's nose.

Alexander saw the mushy projectile speeding towards his friend and tried to drag him out of the way, but he only succeeded in making sure the banana impacted juicily on Melvyn's inner thigh.

Although the manky banana gunk was travelling at the speed of a peregrine falcon falling on its prey, it was too soft to cause any serious physical damage. That, however, was not the point. The point was to add more textural interest to the wet patch on Melvyn's trousers. It now looked for all the world as if Melvyn's little accident in his pants had spread and seeped out from its original site to engulf the entire area from knee to belt. This wasn't just diarrhoea, this was cholera, this was the bloody flux.

'Boggeration,' he said, the nearest he

ever came to using bad language.

'See what I mean? That sort of bad luck – I mean, bad luck taken to those sorts of cosmic levels – well, that counts as a special power. In its way it's as impressive as being able to fly or walk through walls or fire laser beams out of your eyes.'

Melvyn made a grunting sound. It was hard to know if it was a grunt of agreement or a grunt of despair, which is one of the problems with grunting as a means of communication, and the main reason why primitive man invented words.

'So, that's you and me, the first of the few. I'm the brainiac leader, and you're, erm, Unluckeon.'

'*Unluckeon?*'

'Yeah, you know, everyone needs a special superhero name.'

'Unluckeon's a bit rubbish.'

'Well, try to think of something better then. But the thing is, if you and I have these amazing powers . . .'

Melvyn coughed, although coughing is an even less efficient way of conveying meaning than grunting.

'. . . *amazing powers*, then there are bound to be other kids in our school who do as well. Because, you know, it would be a bit weird, wouldn't it, if we were the only ones and just happened to be best friends. So all we have to do is find them.'

'And how do we do that?'

'What we need to do is hold some – what-do-you-call-it? – auditions.'

'Like *The X Factor* for freaks?'

'Exactly!'

Melvyn combined a grunt, a cough and a snort. He was still attempting to wipe off the smeared banana mess when they wandered into their form room for morning registration. At just that moment Matthew Norrington released one of his notorious SBDs, its smell as cloying and fatal as mustard gas.

CHAPTER 11
ITEMS WANTED

The following words appeared the next day in the school magazine, published in both paper and web editions. (The magazine was run entirely by the pupils, with Mr Van theoretically overseeing the whole operation. Mr Van's view – not shared by all the other teachers – was that the kids had to be allowed to make their own mistakes, and so he only ever interfered to remove outright obscenities and split infinitives.)

FOR SALE
Full set of Alex Rider books, unread. 10p. Contact Malcolm Mitchin, Form 7G.
★★★★★
Valuable antique wooden tennis racket.

£1.50. Contact Mary Cunningham, Form 9J.

*****

Pair of spectacles (unwanted gift). Any reasonable offer accepted. Contact Paul Burke, Form 8M.

*****

Oboe. Working but badly stained. £25. Contact Francis Meanwood, Form 7L.

*****

Mobile phone. Can get any make you want. £10. Text me on 07814 568 372.

*****

Scotch egg. Only just past eat-by date. Probably delicious. 25p. Contact Simon Morley, Form 8G.

*****

5 kittens. Two quid each. Will keep till end of week. If no takers, will put in sack and drown lot. Or microwave. Maybe just strangle them. You've been warned. Big Mac, Form 9J.

*****

ITEMS WANTED

Copy of *Grand Theft Auto 4*. Will pay £10, or swap for pair of spectacles. Contact Paul Burke, Form 8M.

★★★★★

Monkey, any species. Will pay market rate. Kevin Williams, Form 9M.

★★★★★

Girlfriend. Must be gorgeous and like snogging. She must not mind clammy hands, acne, BO or bad breath. Text me on 07890 155 878.

★★★★★

Any persons with special powers, such as super strength, telekinetic ability (i.e. moving stuff with just your brain), anti-gravity skills (e.g. flying), controlling magnetism, etc. etc., to join an elite team of heroes to save the world. Come to room 111 at 12.30 on Wednesday. No time-wasters. No loonies. Refreshments not supplied.

★★★★★

CHAPTER 12

THE ✗ FACTOR FOR FREAKS

Melvyn and Alexander were sitting behind a desk in room 111. There was an empty wooden chair in front of them.

'This is the most stupid thing I've ever been involved with,' said Melvyn, his long, sad, resigned face longer, sadder and more resigned than ever.

He wasn't convinced by Alexander's arguments that there were probably lots of kids with special abilities lurking incognito in the school. It seemed to Melvyn about as likely as finding out that a secret tribe of super-intelligent newts lived under the school and controlled them all with mind waves. But the truth was that Alexander was his best, possibly his only friend, and the alternative to sitting here with him was sitting alone in the playground waiting for someone to slap the back of his head.

'I mean,' he continued, 'no one is going to turn up. Even if there did, by some amazing fluke, happen to be some kid who had a special power, then what on earth makes you think they'd want to come and—'

Melvyn was interrupted by a knock, which made his elbow slip off the table, slamming his chin down onto the desk. His tongue was, naturally, trapped between his teeth, and started to bleed.

In the excitement, Alexander didn't even notice. 'Come in,' he said brightly, his voice full of hope, even expectation, that this was going to work after all.

Those hopes were soon dashed.

Felicity put her head timidly round the door. Alexander couldn't stop himself from groaning.

'Hello, Felithity,' said Melvyn, the wound to his tongue making him lisp.

Felicity looked almost as disappointed as Alexander. 'Am I in the right place for the audition?'

'Audition? This isn't *Britain's Got Talent*, you know,' Alexander said brusquely. 'You did read the advert, didn't you?'

'Well, yes, but I wasn't expecting . . .'

'Us?' said Alexander. 'Who did you think it was going to be? MI5?'

'No need to be tharcathtic,' thaid – I mean said – Melvyn. 'If we're going to do this we should keep an open mind.' He dabbed at his tongue with the clean white hankie his mother gave him every morning.

Alexander sighed. 'OK, OK. Just show us what you can do, Felicity.'

Felicity squeezed her body through the half-open door, as if too meek to dare to open it fully.

'We're waiting,' said Alexander finally, drumming his fingers on the dusty desktop.

Felicity looked down at the floor and up at the ceiling, and then at each of the walls in turn. Then it all gushed out of her.

'Look, I can't really do anything special, but I'm very, very organized. And quite often when you have a hero with special powers there's someone else who helps them who hasn't got special powers, but that doesn't mean they aren't awfully useful. There's Batman's butler, and, erm, Renfield . . .'

'Renfield?'

'Yes, well, he's a sort of madman who helps Count Dracula, and even if you say that Dracula wasn't really a hero—'

'Which he most definitely was not.'

'– you still have to admit that he had special powers, such as being able to turn into a bat or a wolf and—'

'Sucking perfectly innocent people's blood, thereby turning them into either corpses or other bloodsuckers as evil as himself?'

'And I can file things and help in all sorts of ways. Everyone knows I've got the neatest writing in the whole school, even better than most of the teachers, which is why I always get picked when someone has to come up and write on the whiteboard. And,' she said, finally running out of breath, 'I've brought my own sandwiches.'

Alexander sighed. He wasn't usually unkind. The opposite, in fact. But Felicity just wasn't what he had in mind when it came to saving the world.

'I'm sorry,' he began, meaning to continue with the nicest sort of brush-off he could manage, emphasizing such things as the danger and difficulty of their task, the mighty challenges, the awesome responsibilities, and the fact that just being good at filing things away and having neat writing and bringing your own sandwiches really wasn't enough to make you much of a superhero, or even a superhero apprentice.

But he didn't get the chance to say any of that.

'OK,' said Melvyn.

'What?' hissed Alexander.

'She'll be handy to have about the place,' Melvyn whispered back. 'And she's right about the superheroes needing someone normal to help them.'

'But it's *Felicity*. Dorky Felicity. If she's in, then we won't be a league of superheroes, but a league of dorks.'

'I may not be a superhero, but I'm not deaf,' said Felicity.

'She's no more of a dork than we are,' said Melvyn.

'Gee, thanks,' said Felicity. 'I think that's what they call damning with faint praise.'

She was putting on a brave face, but both boys realized that she was on the verge of tears.

Alexander sighed. 'What kind of sandwiches have you got?'

'Cheese and tomato. And I've got some crisps. And an orange.'

'What flavour?'

'Orange flavour, of course, silly.'

'No, the crisps.'

'Oh, sorry, ha ha, salt and vinegar.'

'OK, Felicity. You can join as our official secretary. On a trial basis, that is. And if you develop any special powers later on, then maybe you can get promoted to one of our combat squads.'

Felicity let out a squeal of delight. 'Can I start now?'

'Now? I'm not—'

'It would actually be quite useful,' said Melvyn. 'She can keep the minutes of the meeting. Take notes. Write down names. That sort of thing.'

And before Alexander could do anything about it, Felicity had whipped out a writing pad and a pencil case, and skipped round to their side of the table.

She was just in time, as at that precise moment there came the second knock on the door of room 111.

CHAPTER 13
HARRY POTTER, I THINK NOT

'Enter,' said Alexander, with just a little less enthusiasm than the first time, and the door creaked open.

Where they expected to see a head, there was nothing. The head appeared roughly where you might expect a belly button to be. It was time for Alexander's second groan of the day.

'Hello, Titch,' said Melvyn, polite as ever.

Titch Williams was the smallest kid in the school. If he'd been any smaller he'd have been snapped up by a circus, or per-haps kidnapped by the military for special training as a micro-spy, able to crawl through cat-flaps and wriggle up drain-pipes. Although microscopic, Titch was known to be rather fierce. He'd once severely bitten the legs of a stout Year Nine girl who'd pushed him over in the playground.

'Right then, Titch,' said Alexander. 'What can you do for us?'

Titch reached inside his blazer. 'Pick a card, any card,' he said, thrusting a clumsily fantailed pack towards them.

'I don't think you've quite got what this is all about, Titch.'

'What do you mean?'

'I mean, it's not like a . . . like a pantomime.'

'Look,' growled Titch, 'the advert said special powers, and I have got special powers.'

'What special powers?'

'Magic, obviously, dumb-ass.'

'OK, OK, don't get your knickers in a twist. You've started so you may as well finish.'

'Like I said, pick a card, any card.'

Once more the pack was thrust towards

Alexander. There was a card right in the middle that was sticking out a bit more than the others. It was pretty obvious that Titch wanted him to pick that one. Alexander selected another from nearer the outside. It was the six of clubs.

Titch looked furious. 'You've picked the wrong one, dummy.'

'How can there be a wrong one? I thought you were magic?'

'Fine. Whatever. Put it back then.'

'Shouldn't you have your eyes closed or something?'

Titch tutted, and half closed his eyes.

Alexander put the card back in the pack.

Titch opened his eyes again. 'Is this your card?'

It was the queen of diamonds.

'No.'

'Oh.'

He went through the pack and found another. 'Is this your card?'

Three of hearts.

'No.'

The procedure was repeated.

'Is this your card?'

Finally Titch had it.

'Yes, that's it. Amazing.'

Titch smiled broadly and bowed.

There followed more tricks, some involving string, some coins. All were rubbish.

'That was really great, Titch,' said Melvyn when it was obvious he'd finished his act. 'We'll, er, let you know.'

Titch bowed and swept out of the room.

'Not exactly Harry Potter, was it?' said Alexander.

And without Titch's inhibiting presence, the three of them finally collapsed into spluttering laughter.

CHAPTER 14

SUPERSTRONG

The door burst violently open, and a ball of raw energy exploded into room 111.

'SUPERSTRONG!'

The startled expressions on the faces of Alexander, Melvyn and Felicity were transformed into broad smiles.

'Hi, Jamie.'

'SUPERSTRONG!' said Jamie again. He was holding the sheet from the school newspaper with the ad for heroes.

Jamie had Down's syndrome. He was big and friendly and enjoyed everything he did, from getting up in the morning to going to bed at night. Nearly everyone in the school liked him, and he liked them all back.

The other three exchanged glances.

'What can we do for you, Jamie?' said Alexander.

'I'm superstrong,' said Jamie, by way of an answer. He showed his biceps like a body builder.

'Heck, yes, I know you are, Jamie.'

'So, in your gang? Hurray, yippee! Gonna tell everyone.'

Jamie's open face was so full of hope it made Alexander's heart ache. He looked at the others again.

'Can't we let him join?' said Melvyn. 'He is really quite strong. He's the only kid in our year who can throw the shot put more than twenty centimetres.'

'And Big Mac's frightened of him,' Felicity added. 'He always runs away whenever Jamie turns up, ever since Jamie gave him that hug and nearly broke his back.'

'But you heard him. He'll tell everyone.'

'Not if we tell him it's a secret. He can keep secrets.'

'No, look, it's not fair on Jamie. We don't

know what's ahead of us. This might get dangerous. Jamie could get hurt. How would we explain it to his mum and dad?'

The others nodded. It was hard to fault Alexander's reasoning.

Alexander got up and went over to Jamie, putting his arm around his broad shoulders. 'Listen, Jamie, this is just a silly club. It's just a game we're playing. I think you'll find it boring.'

'I like games. Is it because I'm special? Is that why I can't play?'

Alexander was guiding Jamie towards the door. 'No, Jamie, it's just that . . .' But he couldn't think of anything else to say. 'I'll talk to you about it later, OK?'

'OK,' said Jamie sadly as he walked away from room 111.

CHAPTER 15
THE HUMAN HURRICANE

'I feel like a heel,' said Alexander, hoping the others would say something like, 'Well, it's probably for the best,' or 'I'm sure you've done the right thing.' But they didn't say anything. There are times, thought Alexander, when being the leader really sucks.

Luckily, they didn't have time to sink too far into the depths of despond because there came a lazy knocking at the door. More a sort of tired slap, in fact, than a knock.

It was a Year Eight kid they recognized but whose name they didn't know. He was tall and skinny and had a long fringe covering most of his face, but not enough to disguise the fact that he had the worst case of acne they'd ever seen. He came in with long, slow, clumsy strides and sat in the chair, looking like a giant stick insect in need of a haircut and zit cream.

'Hi,' he said. 'I'm Ed.'

There was no way of telling who he was looking at because of the fringe.

'Hi,' said Melvyn, Alexander and Felicity.

'You want kids with special powers, yeah?'

The boy spoke in a lazy, drawling kind of way, as though he had a mouth full of Blu-Tack.

'Yeah.'

'You want to see what I can do?'

'Sure.'

Alexander had started eating one of his sandwiches, and Felicity was peeling her orange-flavoured orange. Melvyn had poured a cup of chicken noodle soup from his flask.

'This is better if I have someone on the piano.'

'Piano . . . ?'

'Yeah, you know, as an accompaniment. It's usually my aunt Gwendolyn. You know, at Christmas and birthdays. Family get-togethers.'

Alexander rolled his eyes. They'd got another one. He bit into his sandwich. Some kind of meat paste. Pink, with a taste like snogging a pig. He'd have to have a word with his dad, who usually made his sandwiches.

Then the kid began.

He made a throat-clearing noise, although Alexander wasn't sure if the noise actually came from his throat, and then he was singing *God Save the Queen*. Except this wasn't singing like any they had ever heard before. Most of the words were belched with terrific force, so that the three kids behind the desk actually felt the wind on their faces. And each time the word 'Queen' came round, the kid would lift up one of his butt-cheeks and blast out a fart. Except the fart actually sounded like 'Queen'. So it was like this:

> *Belch belch belch belchy-faaart,*
> *Belch belch belch belchy-faaart,*
> *Belch belch belch fart.*
> *Belch belch belch belchy-belch,*
> *Belch belch belch belchy-belch,*
> *Belch belch belch belchy-belch,*
> *Be-elch belch belch faaaaaaaart.*

But sadly, that can't convey the extraordinary truth that you could still hear the actual words through the rasping burps and bum-rumbles. It was a breathtaking performance, and it really deserved a round of applause.

Unfortunately the three judges were too busy waving their hands in front of their noses, gasping, retching and groaning, to even think about applauding. The air in the room was filled with a smell like burning hair. Their eyes were stinging, and it looked for a while as if Felicity was going to be sick, and one Technicolor yawn would almost certainly have set off the other two, resulting in a considerable amount of vomit – probably a third of a bucketful, which is a lot of puke when all's said and done.

No one was going to be eating any sandwiches or soup after that.

'I'm not sure what smelled worse, the farts or the burps,' said Alexander, gagging.

The burpy-farty kid sat there with a proud look on his face (at least that part of it that was visible beneath the fringe) – an expression not unlike that of a precocious two-year-old who's just learned to pooh in his potty and is showing the results to his mummy.

'So,' he said, 'did I pass? Am I in?'

'We'll let you know,' said Alexander.

CHAPTER 16
THE LAST OF HIS RACE

The three of them were still standing on a table under one of the small high windows (the only one that opened), trying to suck breathable air into their lungs, when the next knock came.

The boy who entered was vaguely familiar to them. He had ginger hair and round glasses and ears that looked like they'd been put on upside down. There was a very large bulge in his blazer pocket.

'Hello, I'm Malcolm Nix,' he said. 'I'm here to join your organization.'

'Hi, Malcolm,' Alexander replied as cheerfully as he could. 'What's your superpower?'

'I'm a shapeshifter.'

'He's a nutter,' Alexander whispered to Melvin.

'How interesting,' said Felicity. 'What sort of shapes can you shift into?'

'I have the power to transform into anything I like.'

'That's cool. Go on then.'

'Oh, don't worry, I will. But I must tell you that we shapeshifters can only shift our shapes when nobody is looking at us. Right, I shall begin. Please all close your eyes.'

'Is this really necessary?' groaned Alexander.

'There may be an energy burst which can cause temporary or even permanent blindness. If not death.'

'Oh, give him a chance,' said Felicity.

Alexander tutted and shut his eyes.

There was a straining noise that sounded like someone having an unhappy time in the lavatory.

Then they heard a voice that sounded ancient and croaky.

'Transformation complete.'

They opened their eyes and saw that Malcolm Nix was no longer sitting on the chair. In his place was a medium-sized, rather glum-looking tortoise.

'What the . . . ?' said Melvyn.

Felicity added an, 'Oh my gosh.'

Only Alexander was unimpressed. From his slightly different angle he could just see the edge of Malcolm Nix's blazer sticking out from behind a cupboard in the corner of the room.

'OK, Malcolm,' he said, 'transform back now. You've totally proved what special powers you have.'

'Shut your eyes first, for your own protection,' came a voice, which did – to give Malcolm the credit he was due – sound more or less what you'd expect a tortoise to sound like if it could speak English.

Then Alexander did a little mime, explaining that they should only pretend to keep their eyes shut for the reverse metamorphosis. Which meant that they all saw Malcolm sneak stealthily back to the chair, return the tortoise to the inside pocket of his blazer and sit down.

'You can open your eyes now,' he said, forgetting, until halfway through, to change back from his tortoise voice.

'That was one of the most amazing things I've ever seen,' said Alexander.

Malcolm smiled proudly. Or was it smugly?

'Just one question, though,' Alexander continued. 'Could you show me what's in your pocket? That one there?' He pointed to the bulge.

'That? It's my, um, wallet. Yes, wallet,' Malcolm replied rapidly.

'Very thick wallet,' said Felicity. 'What a lot of money you must have.' She sounded like she was enjoying herself.

Nice Melvyn couldn't stand it any more.

'Oh, come on, Malcolm, we saw what

you did. You brought a tortoise in and then put it on the chair while you hid.'

'Did not!'

'Did!'

Then Alexander got up and, before Malcolm could stop him, reached into his blazer and pulled out the tortoise.

'What's this then?'

'It's a tortoiseshell wallet.'

'It's alive. It's moving. Where do you keep your money and bus pass? Up its bum?'

'He's sweet,' said Felicity, reaching over to stroke the passive tortoise's nose. 'What's he called?'

'Cedric.'

'I don't care what it's called,' said Alexander sternly. 'Put this thing back in your pocket and go away.'

Without another word, Malcolm Nix grabbed back his tortoise and ran out of room 111.

CHAPTER 17
REALLY ANNOYING GIRL

'I know what you're finking. And I know exactly what you're gonna say next.'

The girl standing in front of them now had a face as hard and brittle and pink as seaside rock.

'Really . . . well, that's quite a power – I mean, mind-reading, if you can actually do it,' said Alexander, sounding sceptical.

The girl, whose name was Esther Buttle, had come straight into the room without knocking, and just started talking. Hers was not a beautiful voice. When she opened her mouth, the sound that emerged somehow managed to squeak like a rusty mouse, squawk like a tortured parrot, shriek like a monkey, and honk like a goose.

'I knew,' said Esther triumphantly, 'that you was gonna say that.'

'What?' Puzzled.

'I knew you was gonna say that. What you just said, then, I knew you was gonna say it.'

'But you're just saying that.' Slightly annoyed.

'And I knew you was gonna say that.'

'No you didn't.' Annoyed.

'I knew you was gonna say that. Exactly that, in them words.'

'Whatever I say, you'll pretend you knew.' Very annoyed.

'I knew you was gonna say that.'

'You're cheating!' Enraged.

'I knew you was gonna say that.'

'Prove it!' Disgusted.

'I knew you was gonna say that.'

'Elvis Presley jumbo sausage roll Moby Dick biscuit barrel, nim-nim-nim-nim-wim-bim-nim-bim-lim.' Silly.

'I knew you was gonna say that.'

'I'm going to kill her.' Resolved.

'I knew you was gonna say that.'

'Not if I kill her first,' said Felicity, joining in.

Melvyn was, weirdly, enjoying it. 'I think we should let her in,' he chuckled. 'She'll irritate the hell out of our enemies.'

'I knew he was gonna say that,' said Esther.

'It's not worth it,' said Alexander.

'I knew you was gonna say that.'

'Get out, please.'

'I knew you was gonna say that.'

'OUT!' Alexander was shaking with rage. He searched about for something to throw at Esther.

'No need to shout. And I knew you was gonna say that.'

'NOW!' His hand closed around a meat-paste sandwich.

'So am I a member of your stupid gang or not then?'

'We'll let you know.'

'I knew you was gonna say that.'

The sandwich splatted against the closing door.

'I knew you was gonna do that,' said the voice, diminishing as it floated off down the corridor.

CHAPTER 18
THE RETURN OF TORTOISE BOY

Ten minutes slipped past without any more psychos, nutters, weirdos, freaks, mutants, idiots or, for that matter, superheroes turning up. Lunch hour was almost over, and it was time to go to their afternoon lessons.

'So, what do you reckon?' said Alexander, in a sensible, summing-up sort of way.

'I—' began Melvyn, but never got any further, for at that moment the door burst open, and a terrifying demon, a whirling, caterwauling ginger menace was upon them.

'*AAAAAIIIIIIEEEEEEEAAAAHHHH-HHH!*'

Felicity screamed.

So did Alexander.

Melvyn cringed down behind the big desk, his arms crossed in the classic useless blocking position, adopted by the bullied and terrorized from time immemorial.

For about a second.

Then they realized who it was. Not a demon, but Malcolm Nix. He rushed towards them, a look of devilish malice on his face. His right hand was raised above his head, as if he were about to strike them a blow with a terrible weapon – a huge mace perhaps, or a battle-axe, or Thor's hammer.

What he held in his hand was the tortoise.

Malcolm continued his onward rush, leaped, panther-like, onto the desk, fell, clown-like, back on the floor, climbed, goat-like, back on the desk, and stood there, towering above the other three, the tortoise still in his hand, its scaly arms and legs fully retracted, as if the reptile knew the grisly fate that awaited it.

'What the heck are you playing at, Nix?' said Alexander, rapidly recovering his limited cool.

Malcolm was still in berserker-mode.

'*AAAAAHHHHHHH!*' he bellowed. 'I'M THE FAMOUS TORTOISE BOY. PREPARE TO BE BATTERED BY THE MIGHTY TORTOISE OF DEATH.'

'Are you seriously suggesting,' said Melvyn, 'that you're going to hit us with . . . what's his name?'

'Cedric,' said Felicity. 'And he'd better not or I'll tell the RSPCA. Hitting people with tortoises is against the law.'

Malcolm climbed down from the desk. 'You were worried though, weren't you?' he said. 'I mean, when I first came in. You were terrified I was going to smite you with Cedric.'

'*Smite?* Have you been sniffing the Tippex again?' said Alexander. 'It was a bit of a surprise, that's all.'

'But surprise is the most important thing

in a battle. I could be your shock weapon. Like Hannibal's elephants.'

'What are you on about?'

'Hannibal. When he fought the Romans. We did it in history.'

'An elephant's one thing, and, er, Cedric's quite another. What would happen if he got broken when you hit someone with him?'

'I know he's prepared to make the ultimate sacrifice.'

'Fine, but then you've used him up. You're out of ammo. What next?'

Malcolm's face became crafty. 'I've got a spare one.'

'A spare tortoise? Like a spare tyre? Malcolm, you're nuts. You should be getting some kind of help.'

'Cedric's got a sister, Wendy.'

'Oh, and you think this Wendy would be prepared to work with you after you've smashed her brother to a bloody pulp?'

'She wouldn't have to know. I could tell her that Cedric ran away.'

'What, he was too quick for you, was he?'

'So,' said Malcolm, ignoring the question, 'when do we start saving the world?'

'I'm sorry,' said Alexander sadly, 'but we can't waste any more time. There are important things for us to do.'

'Oh, go on, please let me join.'

'Malcolm,' said Alexander, more severely this time, 'you're a fantasist, and a bit of a liar. You pretended to be a shapeshifter, and then you acted like hitting people with tortoises made you a hero. We can't use you. Goodbye.'

Malcolm almost seemed to grow smaller as Alexander spoke, like a beach ball with a slow puncture. He walked at tortoise speed from the room, looking back over his shoulder. Alexander pointed silently out towards the corridor, and Malcolm was gone.

CHAPTER 19

THE FIRST BATTLE: PHASE 1

Alexander shook his head. 'What a bunch of losers.' It wasn't clear if he meant to include the three of them sitting in the room.

'Definitely bad news for planet Earth,' said Melvyn by way of reply.

'When's the next meeting?' Felicity asked chirpily.

Alexander looked at her. 'Are you crazy?' he said. 'Were you paying attention? I don't know why I ever thought this could work. I . . .'

And then he trailed off. He trailed off because a massive figure had appeared in the open doorway.

'Lovely,' said Big Mac, in that surprisingly high-pitched voice, a smile filling his face like a Cornish pasty. 'All the nerds together again. This is going to be like shooting fish in a barrel. And can you think of anything better to do with some fish and a barrel and a gun, eh? Eh? Ha ha ha.'

It wasn't just Big Mac, of course, but his baboons as well. Four of them this time, following him into the room. None of them were quite as big as Big Mac, but all of them were as foul and meaty as a cheap kebab.

'Just my luck,' said Melvyn, under his breath.

Big Mac glared at Felicity. 'You, Buck-tooth Betty, you can clear off — unless you're feeling like a hero . . .'

Without a word, Felicity slipped out of the room, and her quick little feet pattered away.

Alexander wasn't sure whether or not to be relieved. Big Mac probably wouldn't actually beat up Felicity, but he'd certainly enjoy goading her. He'd once seen Big Mac snatch some poor girl's bag and then go through the contents, picking out anything embarrassing he could find and showing it round to the crowd, while the girl cried and begged. Finally he just chucked all her stuff in the air and strode off like he'd done something heroic – slaying a dragon or capturing an enemy machine-gun post. And Alexander didn't want that to happen to Felicity. He also didn't particularly want Felicity to see what was about to happen to him and Melvyn. The worst thing about being bullied wasn't so much the pain (although that was bad enough) as the embarrassment of being a victim. Still, though, he thought wistfully, it would have been loyal of her to stick around.

The next stage happened pretty quickly. There was a flurry of punching and kicking, and the next thing Alexander and Melvyn knew, they were on the floor, looking up at their enemies.

'Did I say like fish in a barrel? Nah. Fish in a barrel would be more of a challenge than you wimps. Still, one has to make do with the tools at hand.' Then Big Mac turned to one of his companions. 'Murdo?'

'Yeah?'

'How's your cold coming on?'

'Just nice, Macca.'

Alexander's soul quailed within his breast. He knew what was coming and tried to get up. But Big Mac put a massive foot on his chest and pushed him back down.

Murdo was famous for his snot. He was a human evergreen, with a heavy cold all year round, and so there was always plenty of it. His big nostrils had a hard, caked-on layer of green crust on the outside, with a more liquid, glistening layer on the inside, like the devil's own confectionery. Sometimes Murdo snorted it into his mouth and swallowed it, as if it were an oyster. Sometimes he blew it straight out of his crusty nostrils into his hands, and then rubbed it over the back of your blazer.

Big Mac nodded to two more of the

goons. They put their boots on Alexander's shoulders, holding him still. Then Murdo loomed over him. Alexander had a perfect view, right up the nose. He watched the green mucus begin its leisurely descent, almost like lava from a lazy volcano. He thrashed and writhed, but there was no escape. He could see Melvyn next to him. A fat kid was sitting on his chest, slapping his face with a sort of gleeful regularity, like the ticking of a clock.

Slap. Slap. Slap.

But Alexander didn't have any sympathy left over for Melvyn. The slow green snotfall was halfway to his face now, the strand unbroken. Murdo's art was to make it stretch all the way until it touched your cheek or lip – delicately, like a butterfly's wing – then suck it back up a couple of centimetres, then let it fall again, caressing you with his dextrous, attenuated snot-finger. And so on until the filament broke, and Murdo's phlegm coiled like a slug on your face.

Keep your mouth shut, Alexander told himself. Everything would be OK as long as he kept his mouth shut.

But there were four of them giving him their full attention, and what he did wasn't up to him, but them.

'Open wide,' said Big Mac, using his fat sausage fingers to force open Alexander's jaws. 'Dinner time.'

And then it happened.

The 'it' was quite hard to put into words, but imagine a kind of explosion made up of bits of human body: hands, heads, arms, feet, legs, ears, mouths, teeth, along with splintered chairs and tables.

The four kids variously kneeling on and standing over Alexander were blown away. Big Mac was left sprawling, looking up at—

CHAPTER 20

THE FIRST BATTLE: PHASE 2

'SUPERSTRONG!'

It was Jamie, his arms bent in that strongman pose again. He'd come careering into them at top speed, and there was really quite a lot of Jamie.

And there was something else.

Big Mac and his mates were ever so slightly afraid of Jamie because he was different; because of his *Jamieness*.

The trouble was, there were five of them and only one of him.

'You're gonna be sorry,' said Big Mac, beginning to get up. He waved his hand towards Jamie. 'Boys, what are you waiting for?'

The goons looked at each other, and

then at Big Mac. They weren't bright kids, and it took them a while to weigh up what was more dangerous – attacking Jamie, or disobeying Mac. And then suddenly it wasn't just Jamie standing there. Titch appeared in the doorway, his face looking even angrier than usual. The cards were in one hand and his wand in the other.

'Pick a card,' he said, 'any card.'

One of the thugs looked down, and couldn't stop himself from putting out his fingers to take a card. With a vicious fizz, Titch brought the wand snapping down on the kid's knuckles. Then, before he could get over the shock, Titch kicked him hard on the shin, leaving him hopping up and down on one leg.

Another of the thugs moved to help him, pulling back his fist to deliver a crunching punch. But before the blow fell, the lank hair and pale skin of Ed, the Human Hurricane, loomed up, right in his face, unleashing at the same time one of the most impressive, formidable, high-octane, full-throttle, hell-for-leather, resounding, resonant and noxious belches of all time – or at least since the last T. rex let fly after scoffing the last Apatosaurus. It sounded like the bellow of an enraged buffalo, brought to bay by a pack of ravenous hyenas.

It was a whale of a burp.

It was biblical.

It was epic.

BOOOOOOOOOOOAAAAAAAAAR-RRRRRRRUUUUUUPPPPPPPPPPPAAA AAHHHHHHHHHHHHH!

The thug staggered back as if kicked by a mule. Perhaps he thought the worst was over, and that would have been natural, because usually a burp like that is going to empty the tank, leaving the belcher as spent as a burst balloon. But, amazingly, The Hurricane had just got started. He followed it up with four short, sharp blasts, like the cawing of a monstrous crow:

GRAAAAAAAK!

GRAAAAAAAK!

GRAAAAAAAK!

GRAAAAAAAK!

Each one hit the thug like a slap in the face, whipping his flopping head from side to side.

He was out of the action. His eyes rolled up in his head, and what followed was, strictly speaking, unnecessary. It showed a streak of both showmanship and ruthlessness that you might not have expected from The Hurricane. He leaped into the air, performing a perfect half-turn as he did so, and delivered the *coup de grâce*. It was barely more than a gentle breeze, a harmless *phut*, but it put the thug down on his back, just as, after Jackie Chan has pounded a towering enemy, a tiny push from a small child will finally push them over. It was the fart that broke the camel's back.

Another of the goons moved – too late, perhaps, to help his comrade, but not too late to repay The Hurricane with a punch on the ear. But he never reached him.

He never reached him because something very annoying got in his way. Not only annoying, but armed and dangerous.

Really Annoying Girl was carrying her school bag.

Most school bags will contain a selection of books, a writing pad, some pens and pencils, perhaps a PE kit. Really Annoying Girl's bag contained none of those things. What it contained was eighty-seven individual grooming products. There were four hairbrushes, thirty-one lipsticks, eighteen mascaras, twelve small pots of blusher, three cans of hairspray, ten lip-glosses in assorted flavours, three tubes of hair gel, five of those things that open up like a clamshell, with a mirror in the lid and a little pad and some powder, and, finally, a large glass jar of gloopy stuff to help remove any of the above which might have been applied to a human face.

All this weighed about as much as a

cannonball, and carrying it around had given Really Annoying Girl an immensely strong and muscle-bound right arm, so that in her gym clothes she looked a bit like one of those funny little crabs you see on the telly with one huge claw and one puny one.

The bag itself was crusted with sharp-edged glass beads and glittering sequins, and its long handles meant that, when wielded by an arm as strong as Really Annoying Girl's, it was lethal.

And right now it fell in a high arc down upon the top of the goon's head.

'Ow!' he yelped, a look of astonishment on his face.

'I knew you was gonna say that!' said Really Annoying Girl exultantly.

The bag swung again – upwards, this time, catching the kid right between the legs.

'Nnnnngthh!' he groaned.

'I absolutely knew you was gonna say that.'

He hobbled away, his hands cupped protectively around his nether regions, as if he were carrying a couple of over-ripe tomatoes.

By this stage Melvyn and Alexander had picked themselves up. Really Annoying Girl, Superstrong Jamie, Titch and the Human Hurricane stood with them, shoulder to shoulder.

Alexander felt something he'd never felt before. He felt like he was part of something bigger than himself.

Bigger and stronger.

But Big Mac was not yet defeated. Being a serious bully requires dedication and a certain amount of self-belief as well as a lot of beef. And Big Mac was a very serious bully. He fixed Alexander and the others with a hard stare, and began to walk slowly towards them.

The goons had begun to gather behind their leader, and they also moved forward menacingly, even if some of them were limping or cradling various parts of their bodies like bruised fruit.

'I suppose you think you've done something brave, eh?' Big Mac said, smiling the sort of smile you'd see on an evil emperor, about to order his enemies to be lowered into a pit of scorpions and snakes. 'I know you dweebs reckon that if you stick together you can stand up to me. But, guess what? You're wrong, very wrong. You can't. Ever been bowling? Ever seen the pins try to stand up to the bowling ball? By the way, in case you don't get it, *you're* the pins and *I'm* the ball.'

Alexander knew that it was his job to step forward now and say something clever. He was supposed to be the genius. A brilliant witticism, a devastatingly cutting remark, that's what he needed. The trouble was, he was only the genius when he wore Einstein's underpants, and Einstein's underpants were in his bag. And his bag was in his locker. And the locker was far, far away. He tried to recapture some of that slight intellectual fizz he'd felt when he wore the pants the first time. Could it be that some of the brilliance had rubbed off on him, been mysteriously absorbed, a bit like radioactivity?

Perhaps, he thought, if he just went for it, his subconscious would take control, and the brilliance would activate itself inside his brain.

He stepped forward to meet Big Mac.

The smile on Big Mac's face grew wider for a moment. Alexander felt as though two hands were wringing out his internal organs like a dishcloth. He prayed that the clever thoughts would arrive in time to save him from getting the kind of beating you'd use on a couple of eggs to make an omelette.

And then something in Big Mac's face changed. The smile wavered, came briefly back, then faltered again. An unaccustomed uncertainty entered his eyes. Could Big Mac, Alexander wondered, sense that he was up against the greatest mind of his generation? That he was about to be out-witted by a brain saturated with radioactive genius?

The goons behind Big Mac also looked as if they'd seen something they'd rather not have seen, like an earwig in their chips.

Then Alexander heard it. A high-pitched keening sound, gradually getting louder. In seconds it had become a deafening wail.

Alexander turned, and saw.

CHAPTER 21

THE FIRST BATTLE: FINAL PHASE

It was Tortoise Boy, flinging himself through the open doorway.

His face was contorted, so he looked as if he were wearing one of the savage war masks of the Polynesian cannibals. But his face was not the truly scary thing about him.

It was Cedric.

Yes, once again Tortoise Boy was charging with Cedric raised high above his head in the classic tortoise attack position. But this time, rather than looking faintly embarrassed about the whole business, Cedric was angry. No, he was beyond angry. Cedric was enraged. He was like one of those armoured horses from the time of knights –

trained for battle, charging as one with the rider, teeth and hooves carving a swathe through all in their way. Or, as his master had predicted, like a war elephant, goaded and jabbed beyond endurance, and now transformed into an unstoppable killing machine.

It looked for a moment as if Big Mac and his boys would try to withstand the onslaught. They drew together like Roman legionaries in the formation known, ironically, as 'the Tortoise'. But they lacked the shields, the discipline and the courage. Before Tortoise Boy and Cedric reached them, they broke, they fled. They ran out of room 111 like chickens fleeing before a fox.

Tortoise Boy pursued them down the corridor for a few metres, still yelling that uncanny, high-pitched war cry. Then he drew back his arm. He was going to hurl Cedric at Big Mac, aiming for his skull, which would in all probability crack open like an egg. And Cedric, in his state of berserker battle-fury, possessed as he was by the ancient Norse war gods, seemed willing – indeed, yearned – to be thrown, and he flapped his scaly little legs like a baby bird practising flight.

Alexander stopped him (the 'him' being Tortoise Boy rather than Cedric). He caught his wrist. Tortoise Boy spun round, ready to fight even his own side if they got in his way.

'Leave it,' said Alexander soothingly. 'They're gone. We've won.'

Tortoise Boy's face relaxed. Cedric may have looked a little disappointed, his dreams of flight for now postponed. But deep down he must also have known that the job was done, and that there are times when the best strategy is to allow your enemy to leave the field.

Now the group gathered together in a circle, facing inwards.

Alexander the Genius;

Melvyn Unluckeon;

Esther Buttle, the Really Annoying Girl;

Jamie Superstrong;

Ed the Human Hurricane;

Magic Titch.

And now, joining them again, Felicity Secretarion who, Alexander realized, must have gone to round up the others to help him and Melvyn in their time of need.

Each face glowed with pride, and no one spoke for a while.

'That was mighty cool,' said Melvyn eventually.

'That was only the first battle,' said Alexander. 'Our real work begins now.'

And at that moment the bell rang for the end of the lunch break and the beginning of afternoon lessons.

CHAPTER 22

REBELLION?

Meanwhile, on the Borgia flagship, Admiral Thlugg wafted a command into one of the smellocaster tubes: *Nutmeg, pork sausage, camomile, wet dog, wet dog, wet dog, Cornish pasty, badger poo.*

Or: 'Attention to the brig. Bring the prisoner to me now. With a little sweet-and-sour sauce on the side. And a carafe of pancreas wine.'

A few minutes later a somewhat bedraggled-looking Borgia was brought before Admiral Thlugg. He was a quaking mess, shaling and wambling and emitting meaningless wafts of gas from his venting tubes. The marks of torture were evident on his soft body: vivid blue stripes and deep crimson gouges.

'So, tell me, my dear Jlatt,' sighed Thlugg, 'did you really think that you could get away with it? A conspiracy, here, aboard my own flagship? Really, my old friend, I thought better of your intelligence, if not your loyalty.'

'Admiral, I . . . I . . . there was no intention . . . I did not mean—'

'SILENCE!'

The stench released by Thlugg's fury and Jlatt's fear was powerful enough to suffocate a horse, if one had been present. (Thlugg had never eaten horse, and would probably have welcomed the opportunity.)

'You will now tell me the names of your co-conspirators.'

'But I swear there were—'

And that was as far as Jlatt got, because at that moment Admiral Thlugg lost patience, and slithered over him, entirely engulfing the smaller Borgia in his gelatinous bulk. Imagine a plate of jelly flopping on top of a wine gum.

The other crew members on the command deck of the ship were divided between those who looked away, appalled at the spectacle of one Borgia eating another, and those who gazed on, enraptured, and a little peckish.

The conspiracy of which Admiral Thlugg had spoken was not entirely the product of his paranoia. There had been rumblings among the junior officers that the humans were to be reserved for the Borgia elite back on the home planet of TZ789644444 (represented in the Borgia language by the smell of a tramp roasting marshmallows over a fire made from his own discarded vest and underpants). There was also another, more radical, item on the rebels' agenda. Was it really morally acceptable, some of them had begun to ask, to eat fellow sentient beings, creatures not much less intelligent than the Borgia themselves – even if they were as physically repellent as the humans?

It was this, or the rumour of it, that had

forced Thlugg to act with such rigour. The Borgia creed was simple. It had two parts.

Part 1: If it moves, kill it.
Part 2: When you've killed it, eat it.

Thlugg was not the kind of Borgia to look kindly upon a modification of this creed so that it looked something like:

Part 1: If it moves, have a polite chat with it.
Part 2: After the chat, say cheery-bye, and exchange Christmas cards for the next few years, until one of you forgets or you make some new friends, or you just drift apart and don't really see the point any more.
Part 3: Then possibly eat them. But only maybe. You know, if there's nothing else in the fridge.

The conspiracy had not reached the

point of mutiny. Jlatt was merely compiling a list of grievances and complaints, which he'd accidentally left in the lavatory. The list was taken to Thlugg, and Jlatt's fate was sealed.

It was all over in a few minutes. Thlugg slithered off the remains of Jlatt – little more than a stain, shaped, as stains so often are, like Australia.

The point had been made. The scene had been broadcast live to the rest of the ship, smellocasters carrying each sniff of action to every corner of the vessel. There would be no more dissent. Admiral Thlugg vented a long, slow, satisfied gaseous exhalation. It smelled of Jlatt. And cheese.

CHAPTER 23
THE PICTURE IN THE NUMBERS

That evening Alexander was lying on his bed, mulling over the events of the day: the distinctly strange recruitment campaign, the first titanic battle, the way they'd become a team, forged in the heat of war. And of course there was the added bonus that they would never have to worry about Big Mac again. Yes, all in all it had been a good day. It hardly seemed to matter whether Otto's ideas were crazy or not.

Then he heard the little electronic tune from his laptop speakers that meant someone wanted to videochat. The only person who ever tried to videochat with Alexander was Melvyn, and it was never very successful. They'd spend about ten minutes getting it properly set up, and then find they had nothing much to say except, 'Well, bye then.' 'Yeah, see you tomorrow.'

He got something of a shock, then, when he went to his desk and saw what was on his laptop screen. For a second he thought it might actually be one of the bloodthirsty aliens Uncle Otto had raved about. Its head – Alexander knew it was a head because it was perched on top of a pair of shoulders – seemed to be made entirely of a shiny metallic substance, except for two deep black eyes.

'Do not be alarmed.'

The voice was grating and metallic, yet strangely familiar.

'Who the heck . . . ?' said Alexander. Then he realized. 'Otto, where are you? And why have you got a load of silver foil wrapped around your head?'

'Otto? Otto? Never heard of him. I am Mr Reginald Fly.'

Then Uncle Otto lifted up the silver foil

wrapping and winked at Alexander, adding in a whisper, 'This messes with their reception. I'm in the computer room at St Mungo's psychiatric unit. We get half an hour's Internet access a day. I've been doing more research.' He replaced the foil mask and continued urgently, 'I've hacked into the NATO Combined Command computer systems. I was looking for evidence of their preparations. BUT THEY ARE NOT PREPARED. THEY ARE NOT PREPARED AT ALL. We are wide open. Like little lambs gambolling in the field as the wolf approaches. Luckily, I have found a few kindred spirits. Others like myself. I have made contact through the Internet. We've been watching and waiting. Some, of course, are cranks. Others are great geniuses, almost matching my own stature. They have confirmed my findings. In fact, they have widened my understanding. The Earth is confronted with more than one peril. The lambs are not just faced with the prowling

127

wolf, but with fire, flood, plague, famine. The universe itself is turning against us.'

'The universe? What do you mean, Uncle?' Something about Otto's tone utterly unnerved Alexander. There was a new seriousness that commanded respect.

The metal-faced Otto paused as if considering great matters. 'No,' he said at last. 'It's too much for a mere child – even if he has the *you know whats* of the greatest scientist who ever lived. All I can ask of you is to confront one evil at a time. Now, tell me, you have the printouts, the data?'

'From your computers? Yeah. I used my laptop to analyse it. You know, convert it from binary, check it for correlations and patterns. And I think you're right. There's something there. Some regularities. But, well, I can't really make head or tail of them. To me it still just looks like numbers.'

'That's because you're using your computer to do the thinking for you. Science is an art, and great scientists are artists. They *feel* the patterns, they *hear* the numbers like *music*. Get the data out for me.'

The printouts were folded up in Alexander's bookshelf. He got them and spread them out on the desk.

'Now look at them. Look at them properly, deeply. Use your soul as well as your brain.'

Alexander gazed at the lines of figures.

'Now, what do you see? No, I mean, what do you *feel*?'

This is what Alexander saw:

```
57595919530921861173819326117931051185480 74
46237996274956735188575272489122793818301
19491298336733624406566430860213949 46395
22473719070217986094370277053921717629317
67523846748184676694051320005681271452635
60827785771342757789609173637178721468440
90122495343014654958537105079227 96892589
23542019956112129021960864034418159813629 77
4771309960518707211349999998372978 0499510
59731732816096318595024459455346908 30264
25223082533446850352619311881710 1000313783
87528865875332083814206171776691473035982
53490428755468731159562863882353 78759375
19577818577805321712268066130019278766 11195
90921642019893809525720106548586327 88659
36153381827968230301952035301852968995 773
62259941389124972177528347913151557485 7242
45415069595082953311686172785588907509838
17546374649393192550604009277016711390098
48824012858361603563707660104710181942955 5
96198946767837449448255379774726847104 04
75346462080466842590694912933136770 28989
15210475216205696602405803815019351125338 2
```

He sighed. 'Like I said, just numbers. I don't really see the point . . .'

'Concentrate!'

'I'm trying!'

The numbers began to swim around in a blurry cloud.

'This is just giving me a headache.'

'As I suspected. It's time.'

'Time for what?'

'I think you know.'

Strangely, Alexander *did* know. If he was going to understand these figures, understand them truly and deeply, then he was going to need some extra help. He retrieved the underpants from their hiding place beneath his bed.

'I still feel an idiot for doing this, you know,' he said to the metal face in the screen.

'Feeling like an idiot is one of the defining characteristics of genius,' Otto replied.

And so Alexander put the pants on his head. He could have been wrong, but for a moment he thought he heard a sort of half-choked laugh emerge from under the silver foil.

'What now?' he asked, a little annoyed as well as embarrassed.

'Look again at the data.'

'It's a waste of—'

'Just do it!'

So once again Alexander stared at the numbers on the printed sheet. Again they seemed to blur and fuzz and drift like plankton. He used every gram of mental energy he had to squeeze the meaning out of them. He even tried to channel his mind through the underpants. He was just about to give up when something odd happened.

The numbers were still there, and yet they had changed.

He rubbed his eyes.

'Are you seeing it? Are you feeling it?' urged Otto.

'I . . . I . . . I don't know.'

Alexander looked again. Either he was

going mad or, yes, a pattern was emerging from the numbers. And it wasn't just that he was seeing some connection between the figures. That's what he thought he was supposed to be looking for, like one of those problems where you have a sequence of numbers — say, 1, 3, 5, 7, 11 — and you have to work out what the link is so you can guess the next in the series.

No, this was actually a pattern of some kind. He was seeing or feeling an image.

Otto had been studying his face. 'You see it, don't you?' he said fervently.

'Something, yes. But what is it?'

'Look again and tell me.'

'It's a shape. I don't know, a blob—'

'Not a blob!'

'It's a thing. It's . . . It's . . . It's one of *them*, isn't it, Uncle?'

'Oh yes.'

Alexander gulped. He felt suddenly afraid, very afraid.

'The next page – what do you see?'

Alexander gazed again. And this time the image came more quickly.

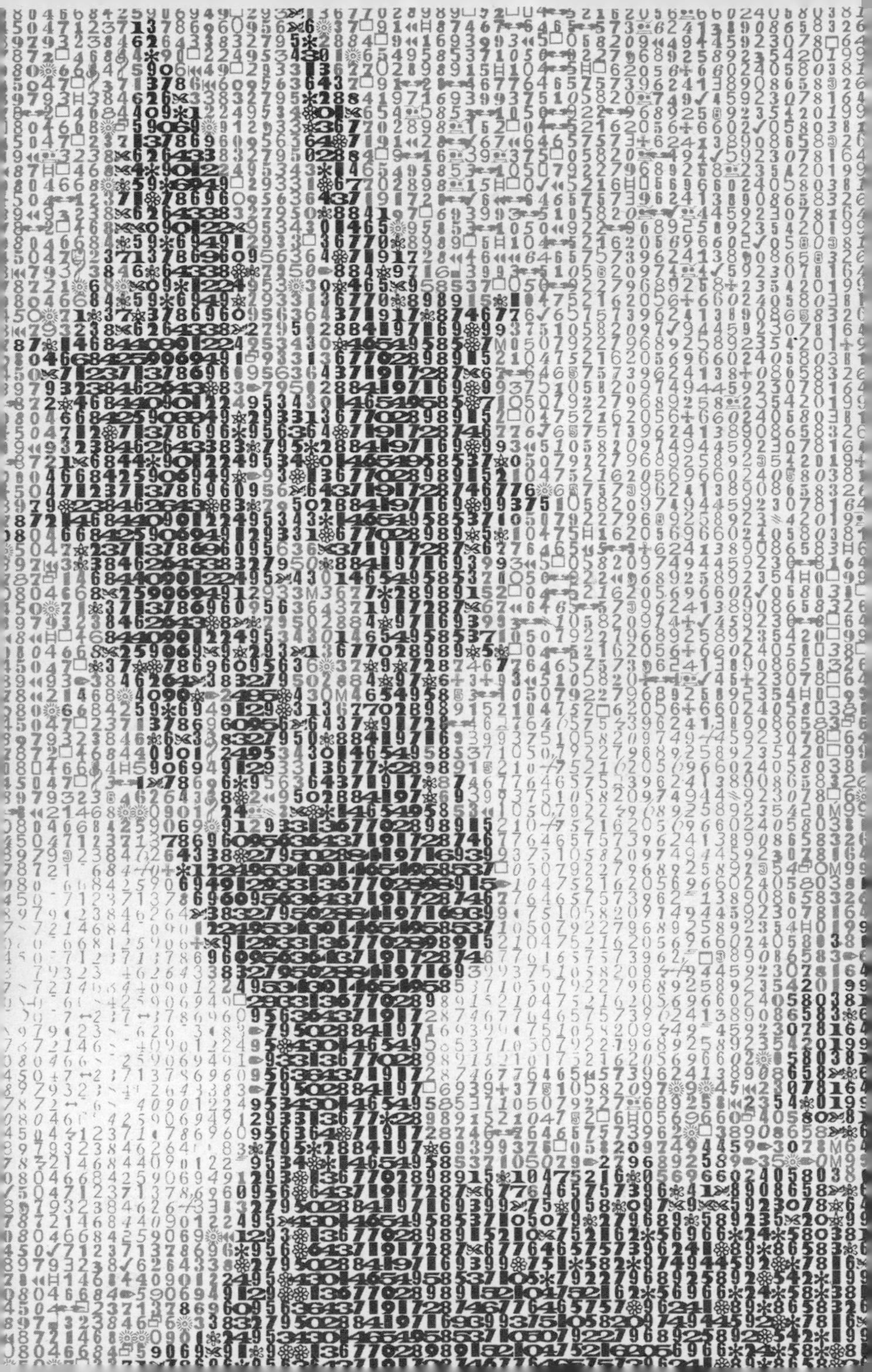

'I don't know. It's kind of beautiful. Is it an angel?'

Otto laughed bitterly. 'An angel? That's a good one. Yes, it's an angel. The Angel of Death.'

And again, as he gazed at the shape in the numbers, Alexander felt the cold hand of fear grip his entrails.

'They are coming. That is their ship.'

Alexander nodded numbly.

'Right, now tell me, Alexander, have you begun?'

'Begun?'

'Your mission. The fightback.'

'Well, yes. Today we began – we more than began. I found my heroes, the guys who are going to save the world.'

'Excellent, excellent. I knew you wouldn't let me down.'

'But I'm not sure what exactly we're sup-posed to be doing . . .'

'Then I shall tell you. You must—'

But then the picture on the laptop began

to break up, and the sound of Otto's voice was obscured by static.

'Uncle! Uncle!' yelled Alexander. But it was too late. The weblink was down. But just before the picture of Otto in his crazy silver mask disappeared, Alexander saw – or thought he saw – another image take its place. It looked like this:

Twelve million kilometres away, on the intelligence deck of the Borgia ship, a young officer sent in her report: *Elderflower, pork chop, pickled onion, old trainer, rotting octopus, new-mown hay, monkeysick.*

Or: 'The human has been located. Electronic countermeasures initiated. Recommend the despatch of a surveillance operative with assassination expertise.'

CHAPTER 24
THE NAMING

'The FREAKs it is then!'

It was the very first meeting of the group, and they had spent nearly an hour talking about what they should call themselves. They had gathered together in Melvyn's garage. It was a good place to meet, as Melvyn's parents didn't have a car and the garage was filled up with interesting junk. There was a fridge, a tumble dryer and a washing machine, all quite dead. There were racks of ancient stereo equipment, wires splaying out in all directions like a mad scientist's hair. There were piles of magazines from decades ago, full of smiling housewives and men smoking cigarettes while playing tennis. There were bicycle wheels. There were mousetraps. There was a box of broken and twisted spectacles. There were two sets of false teeth. There was a dartboard on the wall – although, of course, the darts were long lost. Best of all, there were a couple of wobbly chairs, and a sofa that looked like it had been dive-bombed during the Blitz, so everyone had somewhere to sit.

It also contained a blackboard, in front of which Alexander was standing.

Various other possible names were chalked on the blackboard. Each had a number beside it.

Name Idea	Votes
The Mighty Warriors of Destiny	1
The Justice Kids	1
JERK (Junior Emergency Rescue Kids)	1
KWRAP (Kids With Really Awesome Powers)	1
FREAK (Federation of Really Awesome Kids)	2

There was a general groaning from the assembled superheroes, but they couldn't complain. They had all voted for their own suggestion, except for Melvyn, who had voted for Alexander's idea, and that was why FREAK had won.

Just then the garage door screeched open, making everyone jump. Melvyn's mother appeared, carrying a tray with some glasses. 'I've brought you some lemonade,' she said, smiling.

Melvyn hid his face in his hands.

'Thank you very much,' said Alexander.

'I told you not to disturb us, Mum,' Melvyn said from between his fingers. He had told his mother they were rehearsing a play for school.

'I just thought . . . Oh, well, I'll leave this here for you then.'

Most of the gang were pleased by the arrival of the lemonade, and there was a pause while they all sucked on their straws.

When he thought they'd finished, Alexander cleared his throat loudly. 'OK, now we're getting somewhere. But I guess you actually want to know what this is all about, what we're really here for—'

Alexander was interrupted by the sound of Jamie sucking up the last of the lemonade from the bottom of his glass with the straw. It went on for about forty-eight seconds . . .

Finally he realized everyone was looking at him. 'Finished!'

'Thank you, Jamie. Right. Some of you already know much of what I'm about to tell you, but none of you know everything, so I'm going to begin at the beginning. My uncle is one of the great scientific minds of his generation.'

'Is that the uncle who lives over the butcher's shop in the High Street?' asked Tortoise Boy.

'Yes, that's him.'

'The one who keeps getting carted off to the special hospital?'

'He's much misunderstood. Anyway, he's collected evidence that proves that we are under attack from a terrifying enemy.'

'Terrorists?' gasped Felicity.

'Worse.'

'Dragons?' tried Jamie.

'Worse. Much worse. And dragons are only made up, Jamie.'

'They're in my dragon book.'

'I know, but not everything in books is true.'

'What is it then?' asked Felicity.

Alexander paused, for added effect. 'We're about to be invaded by . . . by aliens.'

There followed the unmistakable sounds of disbelief. Spluttering laughter, sardonic sighs, a short, mocking trump from The Hurricane.

'Man, this is crazy,' said Titch.

'You can't say that until you've heard the evidence.'

'OK, then, show us the evidence, if you've got it.'

Alexander opened up his father's old briefcase, into which he'd crammed hundreds of pages of printouts. He spread a selection of them out on the floor. The newly named FREAKs gathered round.

'What a lot of numbers,' said Felicity. 'There must be millions of them.'

'Numbers,' sneered Titch, 'are just numbers. They don't prove anything.'

'That's just what *I* thought,' Alexander replied earnestly. 'But if you look at them the right way, if you *feel* the numbers, then—'

'You can't feel numbers,' said Tortoise Boy. 'That's stupid.'

Then Jamie sprang up and started stroking the numbers on the dartboard. 'I can feel them,' he said, smiling.

'Thanks, Jamie, but that isn't quite what I meant. I meant that if you look at the numbers in the right way, you see the picture—'

'What picture? I can't see any picture,' said Really Annoying Girl.

'That's because you need the skills to interpret it.'

'Are you saying I'm thick? 'Cos if you are, you are in deep trouble.'

'No, I'm not saying you're thick—'

'But you're saying you're the only one brainy enough to get it?'

'Yes . . . I mean, no . . . I mean, even I needed help to see what was in the numbers.'

'Oh, right,' said Titch, 'so this is the "special thing" you were talking about? Well, I'm not sure if I believe in it, whatever it is.'

'I think it's time you showed them, Alexander,' said Melvyn.

Alexander nodded. He picked up a shoe box and opened the lid. The garage was suddenly very quiet. Even Jamie, who normally burbled away constantly – chatting, humming, singing – stared silently at the box. Later, some of the witnesses would claim that a faint glow came from the box on that first occasion, but that may, of course, have been a trick of memory.

Alexander reverently lifted up Einstein's underpants.

For several seconds the universe stood still. The planets stopped turning. Asteroid c4098 paused in its inexorable journey of destruction. The Earth no longer sailed on its long ellipse through the solar system. The solar system no longer made its way around the core of the Milky Way galaxy. The Milky Way no longer flew from the origin of everything in the Big Bang.

Or that's what it felt like.

Until Jamie said: 'Knickers!'

And then there was no stopping it.

The FREAKs laughed.

The FREAKs laughed hard.

The FREAKs laughed long.

Titch was unable to contain his hilarity and jumped about like a demented flea. The Hurricane's laughter came out as a long burbling belch. Tortoise Boy rolled himself into a ball of mirth. Even Felicity giggled uncontrollably. Only Really Annoying Girl remained stony-faced.

'You are not serious?' Titch managed to say eventually.

Alexander was still holding out the saggy underpants, but now it looked like he was holding out a grey flag of surrender.

'You don't get it,' he said, trying to talk over the last of the laughter. 'These used to belong to Albert Einstein. They have become impregnated with his wisdom and genius. When I wear them I get taken over by his spirit, and I become a genius too. If you put these on you'll see the picture in the numbers, you really will.'

He held the pants out to the others. They all recoiled as if the pants were a spitting cobra.

'No way am I touching them,' said Really Annoying Girl, summing up the general view.

'This is just science fiction, man,' said Titch, waving Einstein's underpants away. 'Leaving aside the whole gross-out side of things.'

'No, Titch, not science fiction: this is science fact.'

'Prove it.'

'Go on,' said Melvyn encouragingly. 'I believe in you.'

'I will.'

Alexander looked each member of FREAK in the face.

This was it.

This was the moment when either the FREAKs, under his leadership, became a force that would save the world, or he himself became not just a figure of fun but one of contempt.

CHAPTER 25

ALEXANDER GOT PANTS ON HEAD

Slowly, and with great reverence, Alexander put the underpants that had formerly belonged to the great Albert Einstein on his head, and waited for that faint buzz of genius to take possession of him again.

It was lucky that the FREAKs had already had a good laugh. What was left was a sort of snorting derision.

'Alexander got pants on head.' Jamie was often the one to put his finger on things.

'Ask me anything. Anything you want. Go on. Anything,' said Alexander.

'What's my favourite colour?' said Really Annoying Girl.

'No, not that sort of question. I'm a genius, not a mind-reader. It has to be something about the world or science, or something that Einstein would know about.'

'I knew you was gonna say that.'

'Right,' said Titch. 'What's the speed of light?'

Titch actually had no idea what the speed of light might be, except that it was fast. Alexander, on the other hand, *did* know. They'd done it in physics not long ago, and, as we've already found out, numbers were his thing. He thought about mentioning the fact that they'd just learned it in school, but something stopped him.

'Two hundred and ninety-nine million, seven hundred and ninety-two thousand, four hundred and fifty-eight metres per second.'

He somehow managed to avoid sounding smug as he said it. Smugness would have ruined everything.

Suddenly the gang stopped sneering and sniggering. Again Alexander felt that he ought to explain why he knew the speed of light, but once more he stopped himself. He liked the fact that the FREAKs were no longer laughing at him. He liked the fact that they were all looking at him in a new way. And besides, without Einstein's underpants he'd never have been able to remember the exact speed, would he?

He could see their minds whirring, trying to find good questions.

'OK, then, what's the capital of Greenland?'

As he asked the question, Tortoise Boy had a sort of sly, cunning expression on his face.

Now, the odd thing was, Alexander had once watched a TV documentary about the Vikings who used to live on Greenland until they all died out in the fifteenth century. They'd lived there for five hundred years, but weren't able to adapt when a mini ice age kicked in, and they all starved or froze to death. The story was exciting and sad, and he'd always been interested in the Vikings, which made it stick in his head. So he knew quite a lot about Greenland. But he still had to dig deep for the answer. What was it . . . ? Nunk – something like that. *Come on, Einstein's underpants*, he prayed. Wait . . . *Got it!*

'Nuuk.'

Tortoise Boy first looked triumphant, then puzzled, then triumphant, and then a mixture of the two.

'Actually, that's wrong. It's Copenhagen. People don't realize that the capital of Greenland is the same as the capital of Denmark, because Greenland belongs to Denmark.'

Alexander smiled. It was a trick question. It was also rather out of date.

'That used to be true. But then Denmark gave Greenland home rule. So now it's Nuuk.'

'You just made that up,' said Really Annoying Girl. 'And I knew you was gonna say it.'

Melvyn, looking at Alexander quizzically, said: 'I can go and look it up on the Internet.'

Alexander nodded, and Melvyn ran out of the garage. The others waited in an awkward silence. Alexander had been confident about the answer, but now he began to have doubts. What if he'd misremembered? What if the pants had betrayed him? If he got this wrong, then it was the end of FREAK. Plus he'd never live down the humiliation. He imagined the scene at school. Everyone lined up with underpants on their heads waiting for him when he got there in the morning. Even the teachers.

He thought about just walking out of the garage, going home, packing a bag and running away to join the French Foreign Legion. Did they take thirteen-year-olds? Maybe he could lie about his age. Pretend he had some sort of disease that made you look thirteen even when you were thirty-seven.

He was still caught up in the daydream (in fact he'd reached the point where he was defending a fort in the middle of the desert which was being attacked by some restless tribesmen, all with grey Y-fronts on their heads) when Melvyn burst back in, carrying a book the size of a suitcase.

'He's right! He's actually one hundred per cent right! I couldn't use the computer because my dad's on it, so he said I had to go and look it up in the encyclopaedia, and here it is.'

He had his finger in the right page. He swung the book open. The FREAKs all gathered round and looked at the photograph of the collection of wooden hut-like houses that was the capital of Greenland. The caption said: *Nuuk (Danish: Godthåb); the capital and largest city of Greenland. Pop. 1,500.*

Felicity gave a gasp of appreciation. She wasn't the only one.

'OK, not bad, not bad,' admitted Titch

reluctantly. 'But it's not exactly *genius* standard. Do something really, really clever.'

'Like what?'

'I don't know, something else with numbers, like Einstein.'

None of the FREAKs, apart from Alexander, was any good at maths.

'What's the square root of a hundred and forty-four?'

Tortoise Boy didn't pick that by chance. It was the hardest sum to which he knew the answer.

'Twelve.'

Alexander knew it shouldn't have impressed anyone, but it did.

Tortoise Boy couldn't ask any more difficult sums because he didn't have a calculator. But Felicity did, in her bag.

'Fine, then, if we're doing square roots, what's the square root of, um . . . two hundred and eighty-nine?'

Now this was another piece of good fortune for Alexander. Felicity had hit on a very lucky number: 289 just happened to be one of the numbers with a square root that was itself a whole number. And Alexander knew his times tables right up to 20 x 20. It took him only a second to retrieve the information.

'Seventeen.'

Felicity looked sharply at him, then tapped away at the calculator. 'Right!' she said, amazed.

'Still,' said The Hurricane, 'it's not exactly rocket science, is it? I mean, you know, any question where the answer's seventeen can't be *that* difficult, can it?'

There was a murmur of agreement. It was hard to deny that there was more to rocket science than knowing the square root of 289.

'Ask something else then.'

Alexander was on a high. He'd answered three pretty tricky questions correctly. He felt as though he could answer anything.

The Hurricane snatched the calculator

out of Felicity's unresisting hands.

'OK, what's the square root of . . . let me see . . . twenty-one thousand, eight hundred and seventy-four point four one?'

It was what Alexander had been dreading. His happy buzz left him, and he scratched his head through the thin material of the underpants. The whole thing was insane, he realized. He had no more absorbed Einstein's genius than he'd absorbed Einstein's breakfast.

Some of this must have shown on his face. The rest of the FREAKs began to lose the look of borderline awe they'd assumed after his earlier feats of genius. The first mocking smiles began to appear. Alexander squeezed his eyes shut, trying to picture the answer. It was no good. He gave up. He said the first number that came into his head as a way of bringing the whole show trial to an end.

'One hundred and forty-seven point . . . oh, what does it matter? Point nine.'

A half-smile of triumph still on his face, The Hurricane checked on the calculator. He glanced at the answer, and began raising one of his cheeks to deliver his verdict. Then he looked back at the grey screen, and his jaw fell open. If it hadn't been attached with skin it would have dropped right onto the garage floor and scuttled off under the old sofa.

'I don't believe it,' he said floppily, because his jaw wasn't quite back to normal. 'He's actually right.' Then he showed the answer to the other amazed FREAKs, holding the calculator to each in turn.

After that it went a bit mental. They all started shouting out numbers to him, and Alexander just shouted numbers right back. After the first two triumphs nobody even bothered to check any more, and the calculator was casually thrown aside (although Felicity collected it later – she wasn't the kind of girl to go around losing things). They just cheered each time he answered.

'Nineteen thousand four hundred and eighty.'

'Hurray!'

'Sixty-four point one seven.'

'Hurray.'

'Six hundred and two point one nine eight seven.'

'Hurray!'

And suddenly they were all over Alexander, still cheering him, but also clapping him on the back and ruffling his hair. They were a team. They were unstoppable.

They were the FREAKs.

They agreed to meet up the next evening to decide exactly how they should thwart the invasion plans of the deadliest enemies planet Earth had ever encountered.

They might have been less relaxed about the whole thing if they had realized how little time they had left.

CHAPTER 26

THEY'RE WATCHING YOU

Most of the gang decided to walk home using the short cut through the overgrown graveyard that backed onto Melvyn's garden. There was a gap in the fence you could slip through, if you didn't mind getting twigs in your hair.

'I think I'll go the long way round,' said Felicity. She didn't much like the graveyard, which was actually quite spooky, especially at night.

'I'll walk you home,' volunteered Alexander. He didn't much like the graveyard either, which his imagination filled with ghosts and ghouls, to go with the stinging nettles and fox poo that were the real hazards of the place.

'But it's a bit out of your way . . .'

'Not really,' said Alexander, even though it was.

Felicity looked at him but didn't say anything, and they waved to the others and set off together towards Felicity's house.

Alexander wasn't quite sure why he'd offered to walk Felicity home. There was definitely part of him that thought it was the right thing to do, probably because she was a girl, and girls needed protecting, didn't they? But then he probably wouldn't have asked Really Annoying Girl. Although of course Really Annoying Girl didn't need his or anyone else's protection. In fact the world needed to be protected from *her*. No, it wasn't so much a protecting thing, even with Felicity, who probably *did* need a bit of pro-tecting, but more a just-wanting-to-be-with thing.

Alexander had never had those sorts of feelings about girls before, and he wasn't quite sure what to do with them. He certainly didn't know what to talk about with girls, apart from The Mission. And this didn't seem to be the right time to talk about The Mission.

No, this situation called for something different. Some kind of light-hearted banter. A joke. Not a rude joke. Something clever. He tried to think of one. What do you call a . . . ? No, what do you get if you cross a . . . a *what* with a *what*? He couldn't remember.

Then he noticed something. Something big and round and silvery. In the sky. He was so befuddled that for a second or two he couldn't remember the name of the big round silvery thing in the sky. The loon . . . the moom . . .

'Moon!' he yelled, making Felicity jump.

'What?'

'Look. There's a big moon. In the sky. Isn't it, er, nice?'

'Yes, very.'

Felicity didn't seem very interested in the

moon. In fact she appeared rather distracted. It was probably the excitement caused by all the momentous events of the evening. She was probably awestruck by his brilliance, the way he'd answered every question . . .

He wondered if perhaps he ought to put his arm around her shoulders. In fact, suddenly that was exactly what he wanted to do. He could already imagine the pleasant sensation of her shoulders under his arm. Almost of its own volition, his arm began to rise out horizontally. It had just begun to brush Felicity's cardigan − with hardly any more weight than a butterfly alighting on a dandelion − when she let out an ear-piercing scream. It was the sort of scream you'd expect from an American college kid about to be dismembered with a power saw in a cheap zombie movie, which Alexander thought was frankly a little excessive, given that he'd barely even touched her.

'S-sorry,' he began, but then he saw Felicity's face and he realized that it was something a bit more shocking than his arm on her shoulder that had scared her.

'There,' she said, pointing to a gap between two houses. 'I saw . . . there was a . . . a shape.'

Alexander stared at the gap. There were two wheelie bins, some cardboard boxes, a mattress and a roll of carpet – i.e. typical urban rubbish.

'It's just junk.'

'Something moved.'

'Probably a fox. Or rats.'

Alexander silently cursed himself for mentioning rats. Girls were notoriously afraid of rats. And so was he. Not particularly afraid, but more than he was of rolled-up carpet or wheelie bins. Although, now he thought about it, there was something a bit creepy about the junk in the space between the houses. He had the definite feeling that the bin was staring at him. It was probably just paranoia. And yet . . .

'Let's get going,' he said.

Now, as they hurried down the dark street, it was Felicity who seemed to want to be close to him.

'There's definitely something weird going on,' she said nervously. 'I thought we were just having fun, but now I'm not so sure.'

'What do you mean you thought we were just having fun?'

'You know, the aliens and all that. It was like being in a drama group.'

'Drama group . . . ?' Alexander found that he was annoyed.

'I'm not saying . . . I mean, I thought . . . But now I think . . . Oh, please, can we hurry?'

And as she said it, Alexander felt a peculiar tickling sensation at the back of his neck. He spun round, almost expecting to see one of the gang there, but the street was empty and silent.

'Let's run,' he said, forgetting about Felicity's lack of faith. They began to jog, but soon they gathered pace, sharing a growing sense of near-panic. Felicity was fast, and Alexander had to strain to keep up with her. Every few metres he twisted to look backwards as he ran. Still there was nothing to see. No pursuers, no passers-by, not even any traffic on the roads.

Finally Felicity stopped. 'This is my street. I'll be OK from here.'

'Oh,' said Alexander, wondering a little if *he'd* be. And then he began to feel a bit silly, and giggled. Felicity looked at him for a moment, and then joined in.

'That was kind of fun,' she said. 'I mean, running like that.'

'Yeah,' said Alexander. 'And what exactly were we running *from*?'

'Monsters,' she replied, and they both spluttered into laughter again. Then Felicity said, 'I'd better go.'

'I'll walk you to your door.'

'No, it's best not to. My dad . . .'

'Oh, sure, fine. I'll see you at school tomorrow.'

'Bye.'

Alexander felt lonely as soon as Felicity skipped away down the street. Lonely and, once again, spooked. He didn't relish the long walk home, but luckily a bus trundled by and, by some miracle, the driver stopped for him, even though he wasn't at the bus stop.

Thank heavens Melvyn isn't here, he thought to himself, imagining the bus accelerating past, spraying a plume of filthy puddle water over them as it went.

CHAPTER 27
THE BORGIA RESPONSE

Admiral Thlugg was going over the final invasion plans. He was surrounded by a group of his senior officers, who were careful not to get in his way. This was the part of the job Thlugg enjoyed the most. Except, of course, for eating the defeated foes of the Borgia Empire. He pointed at a map, using what was left of the cosmonaut's fingers, and vented: *Blue cheese, public lavatory, goat spit, angel cake, fish slime, smoky bacon flavour crisps, aubergine purée, Earl Grey tea.*

Or: 'This insignificant offshore land mass here – known, I believe, as *Big Britain*. That shall be designated a barbecue area.'

He was interrupted by Lieutenant Unguent, a small, nervous officer from the

Intelligence Division.

'As you know, O G–G–Great Leader with the aroma of r–r–rotting Quagg c–c–carcasses—'

Thlugg gave an exasperated burp. 'Enough of your flattery. What is it you want?'

'Yes, O f–f—'

'Spit it out, man!'

'F–f–flatulent one. We have been uploading data from our spysats in orbit around Earth. Following our analysis of the preliminary data, we also sent down a reconnaissance operative to make direct observations. It seems that there may be more of a p–problem with the harvesting than we anticipated.'

'Problem? I understood that Earth military defences were feeble. That they were limited to archaic projectile weapons and primitive thermonuclear devices with no more power than a Clumtach's fart.'

'This is true, O Mighty and Effulgent War

Leader, but there have been reports of special – how shall I say? – *g-g-guardians*, who watch over the human race as a nipherd g-guards his nips.'

'Ah yes, I have heard of these *guardians*. They are depicted in certain sacred Earth texts, are they not? Strange figures such as Mansuper, and the human-arachnid crossbreed, and the one who has the powers of the bat. But did not our experts in alien cultures decide that these figures were mythological?'

'Yes, my lord, so we thought,' said the young Borgia, losing some of his natural (and sensible) fear of the admiral as he was carried away with enthusiasm for his subject. 'But now it seems we have p-proof of their existence.'

'Proof?'

'Yes, Admiral. We p-picked up a series of transmissions from an Earth scientist, who appears to be guiding a group of these guardians – or superheroes, as they are sometimes known. He has somehow obtained evidence of our plans—'

'IMPOSSIBLE!'

'So we thought. But this scientist really appears to have developed a scanning technology powerful enough to detect our presence.'

'Interesting,' said Thlugg.

'And it now appears that this scientist has brought the Earth's finest champions together and is training them so that they might mount a resistance to our invasion. They may also have developed new weapons. But even without new weapons, they possess powers which may impede our progress. For instance, there is one whose name would appear to be Boy Tortoise.'

'Tortoise?'

'A heavily armoured reptilian species. And if this Boy Tortoise can replicate the powers of the fearsome tortoise in the way the Man-Spider can assume the powers of the arachnids, then . . . well, sire, I think pre-emptive action is called for.'

'Of what nature? Remember that we are here to harvest the Earthlings, not to incinerate them – I like my flesh *rare*.'

'Quite so. Therefore I recommend that we send in a combat team to link up with our surveillance operative. The scientist should be eliminated, and the other individuals returned to the ship for interrogation, study and ultimately ―'

'Consumption. Ha! I like your style, Mr Unguent.'

'Thank you, my admiral!'

'Just one more thing, Lieutenant.'

'Sire?'

And that was the last aroma ever emitted by Lieutenant Unguent, as at that moment he became part of Admiral Thlugg in precisely the same way that your morning boiled egg becomes part of you.

'I take it you got all that,' Thlugg said to the new vice-admiral, who was called Xchx (hard to pronounce, I know, but imagine the sound of a mule scratching its rear on the rough bark of an oak tree, or perhaps a hiker's walking boot crunching down on a dry thistle in late August – except in the form of a smell).

'Of course, highness,' said Xchx, without emotion.

'Good. Prepare an assault squad. Send your best troops. Utilize our reality distortion field technology. Make a landing by fast shuttle. Apprehend the Earthlings. We shall ascertain of what substance they are made.'

CHAPTER 28

SOME NEW WEAPONS (AND A WEDGIE)

Zing! Zing zing!

One after the other, the ace of spades, the ace of hearts and the ace of diamonds flew through the air and stuck into the old dartboard on the wall of Melvyn's garage.

'Cooooooooooool!' said Tortoise Boy, and the others all clapped as Titch took a bow.

'Isn't that rather dangerous?' said Felicity.

'*Duh,*' replied Titch.

'I think what he meant,' said Melvyn, 'was that they're actually *supposed* to be dangerous. You know, to the bad guys.'

'Oh.'

It had been a good day for Alexander. At

school Big Mac had seen him walking down the corridor. Usually that would mean Big Mac barging into him, knocking him to the floor, stealing his money, and then probably throwing his bag out of the window. But today, a look of panic crossed his face, and he wobbled off in the other direction. Alexander felt like cheering, but settled for a satisfied smile.

At lunch time the FREAKs all hung out together. They joked and messed about and it was all really good fun. Alexander didn't want to spoil things by hammering home the point that, unless they got their act together, the world was doomed. He thought it could wait until the evening. But he did tell them that they all had to come up with some good new ideas for fighting their enemies by the time of the evening meeting.

Hence Titch's Death Cards. These were thin metal rectangles painted to look like ordinary playing cards.

Next, Really Annoying Girl demonstrated

a new move with her jewel-armoured bag.

It went:

'I-*bash*-knew-*bash*-you-*bash*-was-*bash*-gonna-*bash*-say-*bash*-that-*bash*.'

(It was only a cushion that got bashed in the demonstration, but it still made them all wince.)

Then Alexander got them to learn some elaborate flanking manoeuvres and attack formations he had devised, although it was all rather difficult in the cluttered confines of the garage. One move was called The Wedge, which was intended to cut through closely ranked enemy formations. Unfortunately, when Alexander called out, 'Wedge attack!' Jamie misunderstood, and gave him the mother of all wedgies, which left him whimpering on the floor like a kicked puppy.

It was as he was writhing on the floor that Alexander saw the face pressed against the window. He tried to speak, but could only emit a strangulated choking sound.

'What is it?' asked Felicity, alarmed.

Jamie grinned. 'Good wedgie!'

But then the gang saw what Alexander was staring at. Felicity screamed. Melvyn screamed. The others were frozen in various attitudes indicating shock, horror, outrage.

The face was indeed terrible to behold. Its skin was the rancid pale grey of a re-animated corpse. The eyes were red, surrounded by black circles. The hair stood up in clumps and spikes.

The face disappeared from the window, and the garage door screeched open. The children cowered back. Even Really Annoying Girl looked frightened. Felicity clung to Alexander's hand. Alexander was up off the floor by now, and Felicity tried to hold him back as he advanced towards the gruesome intruder.

'Uncle Otto, what on earth are you doing here?' he said. 'Did they let you out of . . . er, *you know.*'

'*That's* Otto – the great scientist?' said

Titch. 'He looks like an insane scarecrow.'

Titch was right. Otto was wearing what appeared to be pyjamas (although they were so begrimed and bedraggled and bespattered that it was hard to be sure), and a pair of mud-caked slippers. A long, horny toenail had bored a hole in one of the slippers, and a dirty big toe stuck out, in just the way Cedric popped his head out of his shell. He was carrying a shiny metal case, which didn't at all go with the rest of his outfit.

Otto ignored the others and focused on Alexander. He spoke at a dizzying speed. Frothy white triangles of saliva gathered at the corners of his mouth.

'Boy, we have no time. I've escaped. Pretended to sleep. Window. Jumped. That's why pyjamas. Ran like the wind. But they are on my trail. They tracked me somehow, despite all my counter-surveillance measures. Things have gone further than even I feared.'

Alexander struggled to take it all in. 'How did you find us?'

'Your parents. I popped in there. They offered me tea. It was probably drugged. I spat it out.'

'But why did you come? You should have stayed in the . . . where you were safe.'

'I told you, it was *not* safe. Not safe at all. Besides,' he added with a dramatic flourish, holding out the case, 'I had to bring you these.'

'What are they?'

'Weapons.'

'Excellent,' said Tortoise Boy.

Alexander took the case reverently.

Now they knew who the intruder was, the other FREAKs had lost their fear and begun to gather round to see what was in the case.

'You have in your hands,' Otto said gravely, his voice echoing in the garage, 'the weapons with which you will save humanity.'

Suddenly there was silence. Every face was turned to Alexander. Without another word he pressed the polished chromium buttons, releasing the catches on the case.

Click.

Click.

He opened the lid, and then slowly turned the case towards the watchers.

Inside there were three brightly coloured plastic toy ray guns.

The silence lasted another two seconds. Titch was the first to start laughing. The others soon joined in. Jamie snatched up one of the toys and started firing it. It made a terrible electronic racket, a blaring, everchanging *weearrpingpingzwimming* sort of noise, like a migraine come to life.

'SILENCE!'

That was Otto, and he was still just about scary enough to be obeyed.

'Frankly,' he said to Alexander in a deafening whisper, 'I am not particularly impressed by your team.'

'I knew you was gonna say that,' said Really Annoying Girl. 'And the feeling's mutual, you scabby old monkey.'

Otto looked a little taken aback: Really Annoying Girl could have that effect on you. 'You don't understand,' he said, trying to make himself heard over the laughter. 'These guns are special. Our enemies – the alien invaders – are acutely sensitive to certain oscillating sound frequencies. Exactly those frequencies, in fact, emitted by this particular make of ray gun, widely available from all good toyshops. My research shows . . .'

But it was no good. The FREAKs weren't listening.

'This whole thing is a joke,' sneered Titch.

Melvyn and Felicity just looked embarrassed.

Really Annoying Girl delved into her bag and pulled out a lipstick. Alexander thought for a second that she might use it to stab Uncle Otto, but she just used it in the conventional way, on her lips.

The Hurricane farted Chopin's Funeral March.

Alexander opened his mouth, hoping that something clever would come out, some way of explaining everything, of making the others believe in him and his uncle Otto. But there was nothing.

And at that moment the garage door screeched again. Everyone looked round. There were two policemen, a fat one and a thin one, whom Alexander recognized from the morning they'd taken poor Otto away.

'Ah, here you are,' said the fat one who, judging by the way he was wiping flakes of greasy pastry from his moustache, had just finished a sausage roll. 'Let's get you back to the hospital all safe and sound, shall we?'

At the sight of the police, Otto yelled out, 'Betrayed!' and made a bolt for the garage window. He managed to unlatch it and crawl halfway out before the thin policeman reached him and began to drag him back inside.

Then Otto's body went rigid. A new kind of sound came out of his throat, a sort of high-pitched keening. 'They're here,' he cried. 'Here. Here.'

'That's right, we're here,' said the policeman who was tugging at him. 'And we're taking you back where you belong.'

'NOT YOU!' said Otto, his voice now a trembling falsetto. His face was ghastly in the dim light. He pointed out of the window, towards the graveyard that backed onto Melvyn's garden. 'THEM.'

CHAPTER 29

THEM?

After that, Otto collapsed limply. Drooling and mumbling, he allowed himself to be led away by the policemen.

Alexander looked around at the FREAKs. What he saw in their faces was closer to disgust than anger.

'So,' said Titch, 'all this stuff about aliens came from him?'

'Yes.'

'And those manky old pants?'

Alexander nodded.

'Right then,' Titch continued in a business-like manner. 'The first thing to do is make sure no one at school ever finds out about this. None of us would ever live it down. Do you all swear never to mention a word of this fiasco to another living soul?'

Everyone mumbled their assent – even Alexander, who had no more fight left in him.

It was hopeless. Alexander flopped down heavily on the chair and put his head in his hands. He'd never felt so low. How could he have deceived himself? How could he have thought that there was anything special about him or those stupid pants or his crazy uncle?

'Great, I'm off,' said Tortoise Boy. 'Cedric's had enough of this rubbish, haven't you, little fellow? I'm taking the short cut through the churchyard. Anyone else coming?'

'Bit creepy in there, isn't it?' said Felicity.

'Only if you're a wuss.'

Jamie, still holding the plastic ray gun, had moved over to the window. He was firing it vaguely out into the darkness, slaying imaginary attackers. But now he paused with the weapon dangling at his side.

'Them,' he said in a most un-Jamie-like way. 'Baddies.'

'What did you say, Jamie?' asked Melvyn.

'Look – *them*,' said Jamie, gazing out of the window. 'Sneaky sneaky.'

'It's nothing, Jamie,' said Melvyn kindly. 'Alexander's poor uncle didn't really see anything out there. He's not well. There aren't any ghosts in that graveyard.'

Alexander joined them at the window. The light spilling from the house provided some illumination, but it failed to reach the far end, which was lost in the gloom.

'Can't see much out there,' he said. And yet he felt a spider of apprehension crawl down his spine. 'Where did you see the baddies, Jamie?' he asked.

Jamie pointed towards the thick line of hedge at the back of the garden. Beyond it lay the big graveyard.

Alexander peered into the darkness. 'We'd be able to see better if it was darker in here. Hit the lights, someone.'

'Hit them yourself,' said Really

Annoying Girl. There was an unspoken sub-text: *You're not the leader now, so do your own dirty work.*

'I'll do it,' said Felicity.

When the light flicked off, the garden suddenly became clearer. Except that the area by the hedge still seemed oddly dense and vague, like something half remembered from a dream.

Or nightmare.

'Hurts,' said Jamie, and Alexander knew what he meant. Looking at the area of darkness was giving him a headache.

'Weird,' said Melvyn.

'Look, we're all going home,' said Tortoise Boy. 'And you can stop pretending that there's something there, because we all know there's nothing, and you're just trying to freak us out 'cos you're sick.'

Alexander looked round at them. No one met his eye, not even fierce little Titch. He sensed that they pitied him.

'I really don't think you should go the

back way,' he said. 'Otto saw something. So did Jamie.'

'Sure,' said Titch.

Then he, Tortoise Boy, The Hurricane and Really Annoying Girl headed for the door.

'With a bit of luck we'll get home in time for *Britain's Got Talent*,' Tortoise Boy was saying. 'I was thinking about putting Cedric up for it next year.'

'You two coming?' Titch said over his shoulder to Felicity and Jamie.

'My mum coming for me in a car,' said Jamie.

Felicity looked at Alexander, as if she expected him to say something. But he had nothing to say.

'Wait for me,' she said, and left with the others.

Alexander looked for them out of the window, his eyes straining through the gloom. And then something leaped up in front of the window, making him scream.

It was Tortoise Boy.

'Ha ha,' he laughed, holding Cedric up to the window. 'Frightened them, didn't we, boy?'

'Idiot,' tutted Alexander.

He watched as they strolled towards the gap in the hedge at the back of the garden. Whatever weirdness he and Jamie had detected there was gone now. There was nothing but the scruffy end of a garden, and a hedge with a gap in it leading into the old churchyard. Tortoise Boy was at the back of the group. As the others were going through, he stopped and bent to tie a loose shoelace. Then, like the others, he was gone.

It was suddenly very quiet in the garage. Even Jamie looked subdued.

'I'm going inside,' said Melvyn. 'Jamie, you come and wait for your mum with me. You can have some more lemonade.'

'Don't want any now,' Jamie replied. He looked close to tears. 'Are we not going to play superheroes any more?'

'No, Jamie,' said Alexander. 'I think we've finished that game.'

'Do you want to come in and wait with us?' said Melvyn.

'No, I'll just go home.'

Alexander and Melvyn looked at each other silently for a few seconds.

'It was fun while it lasted,' said Melvyn eventually.

'Yeah, I guess.'

Jamie ran over and gave him a hug. Then Melvyn and Jamie were gone. Alexander put the stupid ray guns back in their even more stupid case, and then threw it in the corner.

It was a pretty dismal walk home, with humiliation, depression and loneliness all battling for the top spot in his brain.

CHAPTER 30

THE BORGIA ASSAULT SQUAD REPORT 1

Report

The following encoded smellograph was sent from the Borgia assault squad to the Communications Officer on the mothership: *Lavender, thyme, dead pigeon, cat pee, cat pee, bat pee, sausage roll, lavender, rubber, burned rubber, rubber, spring onion, basil, weasel vomit, used dental floss.*

Or: 'As instructed, we established contact with the surveillance operative and set up base in the quiet area identified as a disposal zone for dead humans. This area surrounded a large fortress with a defensive tower. However, the fortress appears to be abandoned, and we set up our holding unit in the basement area of the building. Following standard Borgia procedure, we have foraged for food in the local ecosystem. The dead humans are placed underground in boxes constructed from the organic life forms known as "trees". Trees are not edible by the Borgia. Some humans inside the containers were fresh. Some were not. The freshest humans were sweet and juicy. Those left longer to mature had a stronger flavour, with nutty undertones, which we appreciated. Some of the humans had turned into a wet mush which could either be slurped neat or mopped up using another mammalian species, such as those known by Earth sounds "fox" and "squirrel". However, many of the storage units contained only the calcium-rich human internal scaffolding, which provided little nourishment or eating pleasure.

'The cloaking device is working well, although as it functions only to dampen energy emissions in the visual spectrum, those Earth creatures with an efficient sense of smell are able to detect our presence.

'Turning to the mission, so far we have

captured and encased in storage drones five of the so-called superheroes. They blundered into our midst as if they positively wished to be consumed. Surprise was complete and they put up an ineffective resistance. It would appear that individually and without their leader, they present little threat. The Earthlings are physically puny, and their weapons are of no significance.

'Unfortunately, the Earth scientific genius known as OTTO evaded our attempts to capture him. He obtained the aid of a number of Earth security personnel, and he may now be beyond our reach.

'The combat leader of the group and three of the other warriors also remain at liberty. However, I am confident that they will be tracked and captured before this planet completes another rotation about its axis.

'I, Under-general Tuuuuurdo Slm, sign off with fidelity.

'Death to all enemies and potential light suppers of the Borgia!'

CHAPTER 31

THE MISSING

Alexander's alarm clock went off at seven thirty the next morning. The clock was shaped like a duck, and it made an electronic quacking noise to get you out of bed. Alexander reckoned that if you drew a graph of all the most irritating things in the world, and then a graph of the most embarrassing things in the world, the point at which the two lines met would be his duck clock.

As usual, he'd been in the middle of a dream in which he was being chased by monsters. But on this occasion there was a complication, in that *he* also seemed to be chasing something or someone else. He was a bit worried in case what he was chasing was Felicity. Did that mean that *he* was a monster in *her* dream? Did the chain go on for ever, each person both the terrified victim and terrifying pursuer?

And then he remembered that he had something much worse to cope with than dream monsters. He had to go to school. He had to see his . . . could he even call them friends any more? Melvyn, perhaps. Yes, Melvyn would still talk to him. But not the other FREAKs. They'd shun him, and he couldn't even blame them for it. And without backup, he would once again be the prey of Big Mac and his goons.

And it was all the fault of his mad uncle and those stupid underpants. Well, their time was up. They were headed for the great laundry in the sky. But he couldn't just dump them in the bin in the kitchen – his mum might find them and then he'd be up to his neck in impossible explanations. No, they'd have to go into a skip or wheelie bin on the way to school.

He pulled on his school clothes. It didn't take long as his shirt was still inside his jumper, the tie loose, but in place, under the collar.

'You all right, love?' his mum asked as they were having breakfast. He mumbled something and carried on staring at the cornflake packet in front of him. And then, with a quick and general 'See you later,' he was gone.

He dragged his feet, trying to put off for as long as possible the gruesome moment when he would arrive at school. It meant he was going to be late, but he didn't care. Or, rather, being late was well down the list of things to care about. A couple of times he approached a bin, ready to dump the pants, but there was always someone around, and he was too embarrassed to get them out in public. He resigned himself to being stuck with the pants all day, like one of those bogeys you can't get off your finger. Another chance to be humiliated.

He sneaked quietly into his class for morning registration.

Not quietly enough.

'Thanks for joining us, Alexander,' said Mr Conway, taking out the register and putting a tick to replace the cross by Alexander's name. Melvyn, who sat in the row in front of Alexander, turned round and gave him a weak smile.

Alexander wasn't sure what to make of that. Was Melvyn's feeble attempt at a smile worse than no smile at all? Was Melvyn perhaps indicating that he and the others had all met up earlier on and had a formal debate followed by a vote, the outcome of which was that he was officially declared a doofus?

Alexander groaned and laid his forehead down on his desk.

After the bell he got up and began to make his way slowly to the first lesson — chemistry with the unnaturally tall Mr Harrison. Normally, the chance to make bad smells and maybe wee into a test tube would have cheered him up, but not today. Today he had to face the world utterly alone. Then he realized that Melvyn was walking beside him.

'Hi,' said Melvyn.

'Hi,' said Alexander.

And suddenly it was OK. Alexander knew that Melvyn was still his mate, and so he could confront the world after all. They chatted together on the stairs and didn't once mention aliens or underpants or crazy uncles being dragged to the nut house. Life was back to normal.

'Have you seen the rest of them?' he asked Melvyn.

'Just Jamie. The others weren't in the playground this morning.'

Alexander felt that prickle of unease again. 'I wonder where they are?'

But by then they were in the chemistry room and Mr Harrison was asking them to please shut the heck up.

At lunch time they went and found Jamie, who was sitting by himself on a concrete bench in the playground. There was still no sign of the others.

'I'm a bit worried,' said Alexander.

That was understating it. His sense of unease had grown into a hard lump the size of Big Mac's fist in his guts.

'Maybe they're all skiving off together,' said Melvyn. He looked disappointed that they hadn't asked him to join them.

'No,' said Jamie, in a matter-of-fact sort of way. 'Baddies got them.'

'What do you mean, Jamie?'

'The ones in the garden last night. Creepy creepy in the dark.'

Melvyn and Alexander looked at each other.

'Jamie, can I borrow your mobile?' Alexander asked.

There was a 'no mobiles' policy in the school, but Jamie was allowed to have one because he was special.

'OK.'

Alexander looked in the address book. 'There's only one number here, Jamie.'

'That's my mum.'

'Do you know any of their numbers, Mel?'

'I think so – Felicity's is . . .'

Alexander keyed in Felicity's number. 'It's gone straight to voicemail,' he began, and then switched to his talking-to-Felicity voice, as it was time for his message. 'Oh, hi, Felicity. Hope you're OK. Can you give me a call on, er . . . Jamie, what's this number? Oh, you'll have it, won't you? Just call me back on this number. It's not urgent. Well, it's quite urgent if you've been . . . but then, if you have, I don't suppose you'll be able to call me back. So, er, well, catch you later. I hope.'

'Smooth,' said Melvyn.

'This isn't funny,' replied Alexander. 'Do you know any other numbers?'

Melvyn remembered Titch's. Again the

phone went straight to voicemail. Alexander didn't leave a message.

'I've got a bad feeling about this,' he said. 'Jamie, please, tell me again what you think you saw last night.'

Jamie creased his brow and concentrated so hard his eyes went slightly crossed.

'Mmmmm . . . sort of funny shapes. Gave me a headache to look. Couldn't really see them because they were hiding. Not hiding – sort of invisibling. But I could still see them through the invisible.'

'How do you know they were baddies, Jamie?'

'Just 'cos they were nasty. And now they got Felicity and Tiny Titch and Tortoise Boy and Cedric and farty bum and shouty girl, and everyone except you, me and Melly.'

CHAPTER 32
THE SEARCHERS

'Right,' said Alexander. 'We're going to go and find them.'

'Yeah, yeah!' said Jamie.

'But we don't know where they are!' Melvyn protested. 'And we can't just leave school, can we?'

Only sixth formers were allowed to leave the school at lunch time.

'These are special circumstances,' said Alexander. 'It's not like we're just sneaking off to the chip shop.'

'*Chiiiiiiips*,' said Jamie.

'We can get some on the way.'

'But,' Melvyn persisted, 'we don't even know that anything's wrong. Just because Jamie thinks he saw something—'

'*Did* see!' said Jamie, offended.

'OK, fine, but then we should tell the police. Or try their parents, at least.'

'Oh, yeah,' said Alexander sarcastically, 'they'll believe us, won't they?'

'You've got a point.'

'So let's just see what we can find. It'll be an adventure.'

Reluctantly Melvyn agreed, although he still shook his head at the craziness of it all.

Escaping from school wasn't particularly difficult. The main exit was watched over by a scary lady called Zelda, who was rumoured to be allowed five minutes with any child she captured, during which time she could Do With Them As She Pleased. However, there was a place where the wire netting of the perimeter fence was loose, and you could squiggle and squirm underneath it, as long as you didn't mind the fact that it would probably rip a hole in the seat of your trousers.

So ten minutes later they were leaning against a wall, eating chips.

'Where do we start?' asked Melvyn. 'I mean, we can't just wander around, hoping to blunder into them, can we?'

Alexander was stumped. He hadn't really thought about what their next move should be.

Then he felt something: a sort of stirring in his brain.

He thought about the story of the hero Odysseus being sung to by the beautiful Sirens, luring him irresistibly onto their rocks. And what he felt was exactly like that. Except instead of beautiful-yet-deadly maidens, it was a pair of mangy old underpants that were singing to him, and instead of rocks, glory awaited.

'Hold these,' he said, handing Jamie his chips.

Then he reached into his school bag and dragged out Einstein's underpants.

Melvyn groaned. 'Oh, Alexander, you

don't still believe in those things, do you?'

Alexander replied fiercely: 'Mel, our friends have disappeared. It's all wrapped up with what Uncle Otto was talking about. And you heard Jamie – there was something in your garden, and now it's got the Titch and TB and The Hurricane and Felicity and Really Annoying Girl.'

'OK, but listen, Alexander, if this all turns out to be a load of old rubbish and the others are just off sick or whatever, then from now on you're on your own. For good.'

He stared at Alexander while all the implications of that sank in. Alexander nodded, and began to put the pants on his head.

'Not here in the street, for heaven's sake,' hissed Melvyn.

'Just gather round,' said Alexander. 'Form a human shield.'

As Jamie and Melvyn hunched to-gether to protect him from the gaze of an unforgiving world, Alexander pulled the pants down over his head. He concentrated hard, praying for that curious trance-like state of genius to descend on him.

'Any ideas yet?' whispered Melvyn.

'Pants,' said Jamie.

'I've only just . . . Wait, hang on. Yes! It's obvious, really. We go back to where this began.'

'The Big Bang?'

'Don't be stupid. Your garden. And it's on the way to Felicity's house, so if we can't find anything, we'll go on there.'

'Finish chips?' said Jamie.

'Sorry, Superstrong, but time is of the essence. You'll have to eat them on the way.'

'You might want to do something about those first,' said Melvyn, pointing at Alexander's head.

'Oh, yes,' said Alexander, wrenching off Einstein's underpants and returning them to his bag.

★

Melvyn's mum and dad both worked so there was no one at his house. They went round to the back.

'Look,' said Jamie, pointing at something in the middle of the garden.

'Cedric!' said Melvyn.

The three boys rushed over. Cedric was lying upside down on his shell. His stumpy little legs had long since given up their feeble attempts to get the right way up. His eyes, however, were open and undimmed. He could see his death approaching, and faced it nobly, without fear.

Alexander picked him up. 'Poor little guy. TB must have dropped him last night. Weird, though. He's normally pretty careful with Cedric. I mean, apart from that whole thing where he threatens to use him to bash people's brains out and that sort of thing.'

'Because of the baddies. They made it all wobbly.'

Alexander looked at Jamie. His eyes were far away.

'He seems to be perking up,' said Melvyn, pointing at Cedric.

The tortoise was looking around at the boys. He poked out his tongue.

'I think he's hungry,' said Melvyn.

Jamie smiled and put his hand deep into his pocket. 'Saved some chips,' he said. 'For special.'

'Do tortoises eat chips?' Alexander wondered.

'Everyone eats chips,' said Jamie.

They put Cedric down on the grass, and Jamie offered him a chip. He looked a bit wary to begin with, but soon got stuck in, as though he'd been eating chips all his life. Jamie clapped his hands, and when Cedric finished the chip, he gave him another.

'He was sick of all that lettuce,' said Melvyn. 'Must have been desperate for something decent. Haven't got any Coke in there, have you?' he added, pointing at Jamie's cavernous pocket.

Jamie shook his head sadly, and they

carried Cedric over to Melvyn's dad's bird bath and gave him a good old drink of water.

As Cedric was lapping, Alexander said, 'OK then, Melvyn, you must admit that this is suspicious. You know how much TB loves Cedric, and he wouldn't have just left him like that unless something serious had happened.'

Melvyn thought for a moment, then nodded. 'You're right. But how does this help us find the others?'

'I've been working on it. We all know that Cedric and TB have a special bond, yeah?'

'Yeah.'

'And tortoises are quite good at sniffing stuff out.'

'Are they?'

'Definitely. I saw this David Attenborough thing about them once. They can sniff water from miles away. And TB's got to have a bigger smell than water, hasn't he?'

'Yeah,' said Melvyn, twigging. 'Water doesn't smell of hardly anything. So you think Cedric could track TB?'

'I reckon.'

Jamie had been following the discussion. He nodded vigorously.

'Pretty brainy,' said Melvyn. 'And you're not even wearing the pants.'

'I think sometimes the effect carries on for a while. A sort of echo. Or like when you stare at a light bulb, and even when you look away, you can still see the image of it.'

'Cool,' said Melvyn. 'An underpant-shaped light bulb.'

'The last we saw of TB was when he plunged into the hedge. So that's where we'll start.'

They reached the place in the hedge where you could squeeze through into the graveyard. Jamie put Cedric down in front of the gap.

'Sniffy sniffy,' he ordered, and Cedric seemed to respond. He strained his long wrinkly neck forward, and moved his head from side to side. Then, slowly, he began to trundle through the gap.

'It's working!' cried Melvyn.

'Hold on,' said Alexander urgently. 'There's something I've got to get.'

He rushed over to the garage, and came back carrying the aluminium case.

Melvyn laughed. 'You've got to be kidding.'

'I'm deadly serious,' Alexander replied, snapping the case open. 'They look like toys, but . . . Well, the thing is, if Otto's right and there is something nasty lurking out there, then he might be right about these things too.'

'Gimme,' said Jamie.

Melvyn shrugged and put his hand out.

'Bang bang,' said Jamie.

CHAPTER 33

GRAVE ADVENTURES

'Shouldn't we put him on some sort of, er, lead?'

Melvyn and Jamie both looked at Alexander and then started laughing.

'What, you're worried that Cedric might outrun us and disappear?'

'They're faster than you think, tortoises,' Alexander replied defensively.

'Whatever,' sighed Melvyn.

So Alexander improvised a leash by knotting his shoelaces together and looping one end loosely around Cedric's neck.

'That is one of the silliest things I've ever seen,' said Melvyn when Alexander had finished. 'It looks like you're taking it for a walk.'

But then Cedric, as if sensing that his moment had at long last come, that it was now down to him and him alone to save his strange unshelled, bipedal, hairy-headed friends, strained forwards and heaved himself through the gap in the hedge and on into the verdant depths of the graveyard beyond.

The graveyard behind Melvyn's house was exactly the way all graveyards should be. The church at its heart was old and spooky, with a high bell tower and gargoyles and odd spiky bits sticking out of it for no good reason except to make it look even older and spookier. The graveyard itself was as overgrown as a jungle, and you almost expected to see a huge python coiled around a tree trunk, or garish parrots flitting through the gloom. A path wove between the trees and bushes, but you still really wanted a machete to hack away at the overhanging branches and sprawling beds of fern and bramble.

Most of the graves were so ancient that

the names carved into the headstones had long since become unreadable, worn away, or covered with moss and lichen. Even the new gravestones of the recent dead soon seemed to list and sink into the mire, and flowers left by the bereaved would wilt before the final snuffle had been sniffed, the last tear dried.

Although the graveyard should have been a perfect playground for the local kids, something about its creepy, seeping damp and atmosphere of lethargy meant that it was a haunt of last resort, the place you'd go when there was nowhere else, when every other possibility for fun had been used up. Plus the graveyard ate footballs and cricket balls and frisbees and small children, absorbing and digesting them the way . . . well, the way a Borgia admiral ate cosmonauts.

Cedric was blind to both the beauty and the terrors of the graveyard. Tortoises are good at putting things out of their minds. They are one-thing-at-a-time animals.

When they eat, they eat, when they sleep, they sleep. And when they track, they track.

Cedric was like a stately galleon, surging through the green waves. He conspicuously ignored the tasty leaves on either side. If there'd been a beautiful lady tortoise, hoisting up her shell by the side of the path, he'd have ignored her too.

'Don't like it here,' said Jamie, expressing the thoughts of all of them. 'Something not nice.'

'I know what you mean, Jamie,' said Melvyn. 'It's always a bit rubbish in here, but there's something else today. Something *wrong*.'

'Look at this one,' said Alexander, staring at an old grave. It was just possible to read the name on it:

MATTHEW WALSH, B. 1848, D. 1860
PLAYING WITH THE ANGELS

'He was only twelve,' said Melvyn.

'But that was the olden days. It's different now . . .'

They looked at each other, checked their weapons, and once more followed Cedric's urgent lead.

In a few more minutes the old church loomed up before them, towering as grim and as dark as a Transylvanian castle. At the sight of it, even Cedric's courageous soul seemed to quake. The worthy reptile's step faltered; his head, which had been thrust so eagerly forward, drew back into the protective sanctuary of the shell.

'They're here, aren't they?' said Melvyn.

There was no need to answer. As well as the palpable sense of evil pervading the atmosphere, there was something else: a sour smell in the air, sulphurous, dense, cheesy.

'Jeez,' said Melvyn, 'that's thick enough to spread on your toast.'

'No thanks!' said Jamie. 'I want jam.'

Alexander picked up Cedric. His work was done. 'Give us another chip, Jamie.'

Jamie reached down into his pocket again, and found one encased in a snug little coat of fluff. Alexander put Cedric and the fluffy chip in his bag.

'Let's check out the church,' he said, his eyes narrowed, his lips drawn tight. This was his fighting face.

The ancient, blackened oak door to the church was set in a stone archway carved with intricate designs. Alexander turned the big iron hoop that lifted the latch. The door creaked slowly open. The only light inside came through the age-dulled stained glass of the windows. Red. The rusty red of old blood.

Alexander did a hand signal, indicating that Melvyn should check the pews on the right, and Jamie the pews on the left. Then he had to tell them what to do using ordinary words, because neither Melvyn nor Jamie knew what the heck he was on about. And then the three friends walked slowly along the aisle, their ray guns at the ready.

As they advanced, the tension crackled like lightning, and the mouldy-cheese smell grew even stronger. Alexander took a handkerchief out of his pocket and tied it bandit-style around his face. It didn't help much with the stink, but it made him feel more like a desperado.

They reached the front of the church without encountering anything suspicious (apart from that stench like Satan's thong).

'Maybe Cedric got it wrong,' suggested Melvyn hopefully.

'No, they're here somewhere,' Alexander replied. 'I'm sure of it.'

They spent another few minutes searching the church. They found nothing. Alexander began to hope that they were wrong.

'See what Cedric thinks,' said Jamie, pointing at Alexander's bag.

'Good idea.'

Alexander put Cedric down on the stone floor of the church. The tortoise immediately started to behave in a most peculiar manner, scooting about hither and thither. He rushed from one corner of the church to the other. Well, rushed by tortoise standards.

'What's got into speedy?' said Melvyn.

'I don't know, but—'

Alexander didn't finish his sentence because Cedric had returned to the middle of the church, and now he was revolving slowly. And as he revolved, he butted away at the flagstones with his blunt head.

'Downstairs,' said Jamie.

'Do they even have a downstairs in churches?' asked Melvyn.

'They do,' said Alexander. 'It's called the crypt.'

CHAPTER 34

GRUESOME DISCOVERIES OF A GRIM NATURE

'*Crypt?* Why do they have to call it something like that? They're making it sound *way* creepier than it needs to be. Anyway, how do we get down?'

'There,' said Jamie, pointing to a small wooden door in the corner.

Tucking Cedric under one arm and holding his ray gun in the opposite hand, Alexander led the way to the door. He turned the handle carefully, and pushed. He had to stand back from the hot wave of stink that flowed out like blood from a severed artery. When the first rush had passed, Alexander stepped forward again. A stairway spiralled down from the door. There was nothing to see except for the stone walls being gradually swallowed by the darkness.

He turned and faced the other two. Melvyn looked scared. But he hadn't run away, and Alexander knew that true courage meant being scared and still not running away.

Jamie didn't look scared at all. In fact he looked quite happy. He was smiling that gummy smile of his. It was impossible not to grin back at him.

But that smile was also the reason why Alexander couldn't let him come with them down into the crypt.

'Jamie, I've got a special mission for you.'

Jamie's smile slowly faded, and he looked puzzled. 'Got mission already. Save Felicity and tiny Titch and, and, and *everyone*.'

'Yeah, I know, Jamie, but you see, you're Superstrong, so we need you to watch our backs. The guy who watches your back has to be the best, because if they get behind us, then we're done for. And you've got to look after Cedric too. You know, take care of him for TB.'

That was the clincher.

'OK,' said Jamie uncertainly. 'Superstrong.' He showed his biceps, but without his usual bravado.

'So you wait here for us then?' Alexander said, putting Cedric back in the bag again and handing it to Jamie. 'You can sit on one of the benches.'

Jamie nodded.

Then Alexander reached into his school bag and dragged out Einstein's underpants. He thought about wearing them over his trousers, Superman-style. But then he thought that if ever he needed their help it was now, and so on his head they went, pulled firmly down over his ears. Sometimes to fight hard you have to think hard.

Melvyn didn't even smile when he saw the pants.

'You ready?' asked Alexander.

'As ready as I'll ever be.'

'Great. Let's do this. And keep it quiet.'

★

The steps of the spiral staircase were worn and slippery and narrow, and Alexander stumbled three times on the way down. There was a thick rope along the wall to act as a handrail, but it sagged when you grabbed it, and was hardly any use at all. But soon he saw below them another low arch, where the stairway opened into the crypt. An eerie green light seeped from the opening, like pus from a septic toe.

There was just enough room at the bottom of the stairs to stand beside the arch without being seen. Sensing Melvyn close behind him, Alexander peeked out. It took a few seconds for him to get used to the strange light, and a few more for him to even begin to understand what he was looking at.

The crypt was about a quarter of the size of the church above it, and it was full of old church junk: splintered pews and headless statues and sections of broken stained glass. But there were things in that crypt that did not belong in a church. There were what looked like complicated electronic devices, but their forms were curiously curved and organic, and they pulsed as though alive. Coiling snakes of plasma tubing ran between rippling screens, and those screens showed kaleidoscopic images and shapes, beautiful and terrible to behold. Alexander was most disturbed, however, by the walls. The stone and brick had been coated with a layer of gently pulsing green slime, like the secretions of some grotesque mollusc.

Nothing moved in the crypt, and yet everything seemed alive.

And then Alexander's horrified and fascinated eye reached the far end of the crypt. A row of greenish shapes, fat and rubbery, glistening like the insides of some dead beast, were arranged against the wall.

Alexander stepped out into the crypt. Without looking, he knew that Melvyn was still with him: neither of them wanted to be alone in this place.

As he approached the shapes, he was gripped by a horror such as he had never known before. They were semi-transparent, and Alexander thought he could see through them to the wall behind, which seemed to be hung with paintings: religious scenes, perhaps. The Good Shepherd; a Nativity; a Crucifixion.

And then Alexander realized that these things were not *behind* the shapes. They were *inside* them. He moved so that his face was close enough to the glistening, waxy surface for him to be able to feel the brush of his own breath as it bounced back; close enough to see his own reflection in the surface, strangely superimposed onto what lay beneath.

And then the shape within the shape moved. A shudder. And then the shape within the shape opened an eye.

Alexander recoiled, as if slapped.

'Felicity!'

CHAPTER 35

THE FIREFIGHT

It was her. Felicity. It was her face *inside that thing*. Not just her face, but all of her. And that eye was now staring at him. He fought the urge to flee, screaming, from this hellish place.

He heard Melvyn's tremulous voice beside him. Until he spoke he'd forgotten he was there.

'It's them,' Melvyn murmured. 'All of them. What's happened?'

Alexander glanced at him. Melvyn's face was ghastly in the green light. Then he looked at Felicity again. Both her eyes were now open and staring at him. And her face showed so much pain, so much horror. Her mouth moved in a silent scream.

And then he saw that her eyes were not looking *at* him, but *beyond* him.

Her scream was not a scream of pain, but of warning.

And at the same moment he became aware of a noise: the sickening slow squelch of something soft moving over the dry ground. And now he saw something else besides his face reflected in the surface of the green pods.

Behind him.

Something looming and monstrous.

Something, in its slow, slippery movement, unfathomably sly.

'*Melvyn*,' he hissed.

Melvyn looked at him, his face still drained of life, of light, of colour, of hope.

'Your gun. Get it ready. On three, we turn and shoot.'

Melvyn's eyes opened wide, and he nodded, although it may have been nothing more than a tremble.

Alexander mouthed the words *one* and *two*, and then screamed, '*THREE!*'

Melvyn joined in on the scream, simultaneously a sudden release of pent-up tension, an animal yell, a savage war cry.

The two boys leaped in the air as they spun, their fingers already beginning to squeeze the triggers of their modified ray guns.

It was lucky that they were. The sight that confronted them was so appalling, so astonishing, so hideous that they might never have found the triggers if their fingers were not already in place.

It was, of course, the Borgia assault team. Eight undulating, throbbing sacs of viscous malevolence, oozing their way towards them. *VEEEEUUUUMMMMSPPPPPUTTT-TTZZZZZZZXITTTTTTTOUEEEEOUE EEOUEEE!*

The wall of noise from the ray guns was deafening in the confined space of the crypt.

The Borgia warriors froze, then seemed to stagger back for a moment. A tiny fragment of hope cut through the horror in Alexander's soul. The guns were working, they were really working. Uncle Otto wasn't just sane, but, like Einstein, he was a genius!

Alexander fired three more blasts – *UMMMMSPPPPPUTTT UMMMMSPPPP-PUTTT UMMMMSPPPPPUTTT* – going for the centre and either flank of the assault.

But something had changed. The shots did not have the same staggering impact. The creatures were not thrown back, not so much as a centimetre. They came on.

The guns were useless. Alexander hurled the worthless piece of junk at the nearest creature. It was no more effective as a projectile than it had been as a ray gun. The hard plastic was absorbed into the soft body, sucked and gnawed, and then spat out.

This was it. The last of the FREAKs were about to end up inside these monsters.

And then, from behind the line of giant slugs there came a roar.

'SUPERSTRONG!'

'No, Jamie, stop!' yelled Alexander. 'Run for it! Run for your life!'

But Jamie was already throwing himself forward, and he could no more stop than an army of rampaging medieval knights could pause in the middle of a charge and decide to have a cup of tea.

The Borgia had time only to shuffle half round to meet the new challenge. Jamie reached the enemy line, drew back his meaty fist and punched the first soft body with all his might. His fist plunged through the flesh of the Borgia like a hammer hitting a plate of jelly.

For a second Jamie's face registered satisfaction – joy, almost. Then it changed. He tried to withdraw his arm – which had disappeared up to the elbow – like a bear taking its paw out of a honey pot. But it wouldn't move. He tried to push against the Borgia with his other hand. But that also sank into the jelly. Jamie was stuck. A second Borgia now slithered over and began to engulf the parts of Jamie not already swallowed by the first.

'Hurts,' Jamie cried out. 'Hurts a lot.'

Alexander tried to reach him, his soul aching with the knowledge that he'd let his friends down — not just Jamie, but all of them; the knowledge that he had led them to their doom.

And then he felt nothing, as a blast of gas from the Borgia leader hit him in the face and knocked him clean out.

BORGIA REPORT, SENT IN TRANSIT FROM EARTH TO THE BORGIA FLAGSHIP:

Muffins, celery, newt poo, newt poo, athletes' foot powder, chicken grease, sausage roll, chemical toilet on a badly maintained campsite.

Or: 'As anticipated, the remaining Earth warriors attempted to free their captured comrades. It was a simple matter to surround them, as their attention was focused on the storage drones. There was one major surprise, which could have resulted in a serious setback. The Earthlings were armed with sonic disruptor weapons of the kind we had not expected in such a backward civilization.

The modulator was set very close to the frequency most fatal to the Borgia. Had the oscillations been increased by two microns, then our mission would have ended there, with our protoplasm splattered over the walls. However, although the frequency was unpleasant, it was not disabling, and we were able to resume our attack. To give the Earth warriors credit, one of them did manage to launch a surprise rear assault, but that was soon repulsed and the last of the Earthlings made captive. We return immediately.

'I, Under-general Tuuuuurdo Slm, sign out with fidelity.

'Death to all enemies and potential light suppers of the Borgia!'

Now probably isn't the best time to tell you about the progress of Asteroid c4098. But it's still coming, still on its way, still ready to wipe out millions of years of evolution.

The only question is: will life be annihilated by the asteroid or by the Borgia?

CHAPTER 36
AMONG THE BORGIA

Alexander emerged back into consciousness at the precise moment he was being expelled by the Borgia storage drone. He felt like toothpaste being squeezed out of the tube. He landed on the floor with a thump, and squirmed. He was covered in a thick grey-green slime, which looked and smelled like the combination of duck poo, mud, dead frogspawn and decaying weed you'd find at the bottom of a neglected village pond.

He tried to stand, but his legs were jelly. He strained to see, but his eyes were dim. He could hear a sound like gas bubbling through water, and a complicated series of smells filled his nose, one after the other, some foul, some sickly sweet.

He could not see because his eyes were full of slime. He wiped them as best he could, but his vision was still blurred, and he could only make out hulking and distorted shapes and a luminous throbbing green coming from the darkness around him.

If he could not see or walk, he could still think. Was this another of his dreams? Would he soon wake to the sound of his duck clock quacking? Or would his mother touch him on the arm and put a nice cup of tea on his bedside table?

But this was no dream. He remembered Felicity's horrified face. He remembered Jamie and Melvyn, succumbing to the brute force of the . . . the *things*. The things his uncle had warned him about.

So everything Otto had said was true. For the first time ever, Alexander wished his uncle really had been a lunatic.

His mind came back to Felicity's face. Where was she now? Where were Jamie, and Melvyn . . . all of them?

He felt sick. He *was* sick. And once he had finished being sick, he wept. The tears washed his eyes clean. He blinked and he saw.

The place was dark, lit only by flickering red lights and that sickly green glow that penetrated Alexander's skull like a migraine. There were intricate banks of equipment, with jagging spikes and jawlike gripping structures. The skeleton of a creature, species unknown, hung from chains. Other bodies, at various stages of decay, dangled from the ceiling and walls, gripped by tentacles that seemed to occupy an intermediate stage of existence somewhere between machine and beast.

Towards one side of the room there was a curious device, about the size of an arm-chair, with a number of funnel-shaped projections at one end and a metal grille at the other.

But neither the strange mechanical objects nor the mutilated remains in the room held Alexander's attention. For Alexander was not alone. Now that his eyes had cleared he could see the vile, shuffling forms of the Borgia, who had gathered to observe their captive, their victim, their supper. But even these ogres were dwarfed by the grotesque and monstrous figure before him.

Alexander was in the private torture chamber of Thlugg, and the admiral was there to undertake the interrogation personally.

As terrifying as the other Borgia were, nothing could have prepared Alexander for the horror of being in the presence of the enemy leader (although of course, at this point, he had no inkling that this was what confronted him).

First there was the stench. It was like being trapped inside the decomposing body of a whale found rotting on the beach. The odour was thick enough to coat his tongue with an oily film. The looks went with the smell: Thlugg's vast, distended body looked like a green, pus-filled bin-liner. The cosmonaut body parts had by now been almost completely digested by the admiral, leaving only a trace on the wattled skin. But Alexander could still just make out the poignant shape of the fingers, the melancholy curve of a buttock, the horrific suggestion of a blind human eye.

Yet it was neither the smell nor the appearance of the giant Borgia that so dismayed Alexander. It was the pervasive sense of evil that emanated from the monster. This was a creature, Alexander sensed, that took immense pleasure not just from defeating its enemies, but from the suffering this caused; a creature that relished mental and physical anguish in the way others might enjoy a good book or a stroll in the park.

And then there were the terrible table manners.

Thlugg was sitting in his dinner. The dinner was in a large metallic bowl the size of a double bed, and the Borgia was squatting on the top. With dismay Alexander saw that the dinner was moving.

And it was furry.

Oh yes, Admiral Thlugg was squatting in a giant bowl of rabbits, squirrels, puppies and kittens, brought back for him by the assault squad that had captured the FREAKs. They writhed and squirmed, they mewled, they squealed, but they could not escape. They were hoovered up, engulfed, slurped, dissolved. When there was nothing left, Thlugg flopped out of the bowl like a morbidly obese man getting out of a bath.

And suddenly Alexander realized what must have happened to his friends. A choking wave of disgust and horror filled his soul.

'You beast,' he said under his breath. 'You filthy, filthy beast.'

CHAPTER 37
A HOPELESS HOPE

He tried to get to his feet, determined to reach the monster and exact some kind of revenge, however feeble. But his legs were still useless, and all he could do was grovel and flap about on the floor like a landed fish.

And then there was a foul wet sound all around him, and the room filled with sulphurous emissions. Alexander was so focused on the repulsive leader that he had forgotten about the other creatures in the room lurking like glistening sea anemones around a rockpool. They were shaking, and the gas squirted out in little puffs from fissures in their skin. A sound came from the metal grille at the front of the strange machine Alexander had noticed.

Ha. Ha. Ha.

A staccato laugh.

For a second Alexander thought it was the box that was laughing at him. Then he realized that it wasn't the box but the creatures that were laughing. In a flash he deduced that the box was a translation device, and that what it translated was the rich language of smell wafted out by the aliens.

The massive Borgia leader shuffled closer to one of the funnel-shaped projections and sent out a puff of gas. There was a delay of a few seconds, and then a voice emerged from the grille. The voice was eerily mechanical. Although perfectly understandable, the words were a little muddled.

'This hear, worm. Thlugg I am, Admiral Borgia Fleet, Consul of the Empire Borgia, Shredder of Men, Eater of Mice and Rabbits. You will information me now of Earth defence shield base stations the coordinates. Then you will speak precise mega-tonnage of warheads in defence shield. Then you will announce me correct frequency for jamming communications of Earth defence force radio machines. And then, only and then, will you tell me secret of good pizza.'

Alexander felt waves of confusion batter him, hurling the fragile boat of his brain about on violent seas. As far as he knew, there wasn't an Earth defence shield, or base stations, or any of that stuff. Humans were too busy fighting each other to look up and fear the heavens. And even if there were such things, how the heck would he know all about codes and mega-tonnage? He couldn't understand any of it. He wanted to be at home with his mum and dad. He wished he'd never had an uncle Otto, never got involved in this stupid mess.

Except that there was another realiza-tion. Staying at home with Mum and Dad wouldn't help. These monsters were going to destroy the world.

And he was the Earth's last hope.

A hopeless hope.

'Or speak die,' came the voice, harsh and grating and annoyingly ungrammatical.

What could he do? What should he say? He put his hand to his head. And there he felt not his hair, as he'd expected, but Einstein's underpants, still damp with Borgia goo. And suddenly his thoughts gained a new clarity. His hatred and his intelligence came together, diamond-hard and bright.

If these things – Borgia, they'd called themselves – if they really thought Earth had some kind of lethal defence shield, then maybe they'd just go off and bother some other planet. Venus, maybe, or Uranus. Because that was the thing about bullies, wasn't it? That they always picked on the dweeb, the weakling without a decent defensive shield – or at least without a big brother who was known to be a bit of a psycho and used to be in the army. He knew it was his chance to really be a hero, to sacrifice himself for the good of all humanity.

So Alexander spoke, aiming his voice at the same grille that translated the Borgia language into his own.

'You will never defeat the inhabitants of planet Earth. We have weapons of great power. We are a peaceful people, but we fight fire with fire, meet force with irresistible force. We will never submit to aggression. Our mighty defence shield will annihilate your ships, leaving nothing but smouldering wrecks to drift back to your homeworld to tell of the catastrophe that has befallen your race. And, by the way, you stink.'

'Brave smells,' said Thlugg, after Alexander's words had been translated into malodorous puffs. 'I was hoping that there would be some fight in you. Means live longer under torture pain, make more big laughs for Thlugg.'

Then the admiral moved away from the translation device and vented some instructions. A little of the gas seeped towards the funnels and some of the words were translated. It was enough to let Alexander know that he was about to set off along a dark path; and at the end of the path, the darkness deepened.

'Prepare . . . ordeal . . . ready . . . equipment . . . torture . . . Earthling . . . pain . . . ha . . . ha . . . ha.'

CHAPTER 38

TORTURED

The guards forced Alexander onto a low table. Metal bands enclosed his ankles, wrists, neck and forehead, so that he could do nothing more than wiggle his toes and fingers.

He was looking straight up, and watched as a wet fissure opened in the ceiling, dropping cold dollops of slime on his face. The crack widened, and a piece of equipment began to descend towards him, suspended by a thin strand of mucusy cord. Alexander quaked to his very soul.

The device stopped a few centimetres from his face. There was a pause of a couple of seconds. Alexander sensed the evil Borgia leader drawing closer – not for any practical purpose but simply, Alexander knew, so that he could breathe in some of the fear emanating from the captive human.

Two prongs slithered from the end of the device. Alexander whimpered, too petrified to scream.

This was even worse than being snotted by Murdo.

The prongs, like two fat green earthworms, wriggled towards his nostrils. Alexander was convinced they were going to bore into his brain, sucking out the knowledge that the Borgia wanted.

The prongs entered his nostrils.

Alexander wanted to sneeze, but it seemed that even the sneeze was too frightened to emerge. He prepared himself for the agony he would surely feel as the prongs burst up into his brain. A moment later he heard a faint hiss, and immediately a foul smell filled his nose. He flinched and tried to pull away, but his head was too securely bound.

Acid, he thought. Or poison gas. Something terrible. Something that would kill or maim, or drive him insane. His mind searched desperately for something — a life raft, any scrap of hope.

He had nothing.

Except for the pants. Einstein's underpants.

Please, Einstein's underpants, he prayed. *Help me. Come to me in my hour of need.*

Another nasal squirt jolted him. The smell was pretty bad. Cabbage, with a hint of egg. Pretty standard fart smell, in fact. The sort of thing The Hurricane could churn out in his sleep. Was that it? What about the acid?

Suddenly Alexander felt the urge to giggle. But he also felt the glowering presence of the Borgia admiral, and the almost equally evil crew.

But that wasn't all he could feel. There was a tingling sensation. The pants were answering his call. The pants were working their magic. Ideas, fizzing and zipping.

This ordeal by stench was obviously considered the most terrible torture by the Borgia. The Borgia worked on smell. That's where they were most sensitive. Perhaps for them, he mused, this was the equivalent of red-hot needles stuck into your eyeballs, or having your fingernails pulled out. No, maybe more like the most terrifyingly loud noise blasted into your ears. And his captors thought it would have the same effect on him.

Right then. He knew what to do. It was time to put on a show. His eyes opened wide, he began a high-pitched keening, growing into a full scream. He strained at the bonds securing him. He arched his back, as if he'd been jolted by a massive electric shock.

And all the while he sensed the lascivious pleasure of the creatures around him. They were like gluttons watching a doner kebab revolve on the spit.

Thlugg vented, and 'Speak, slave!' said the mechanical voice.

'Never,' said Alexander. 'I'll die first.'

The smell was getting fairly noxious by now. If you were at home and your granny let go one of those beauties, then you wouldn't just sit there. You'd either be opening the window or, more likely, running out of the room gasping. But if you had to endure it to save the world, then you would.

Thlugg loomed over Alexander, and a cold dollop of drool splashed onto his forehead.

The 'Speak, slave!' 'Never!' conversation went on for a while, and then a new tone emerged from the speaker.

'This Earthling endures muchly. Braver than kamikaze worms of planet Zomit. Fine. Test let us how he wants cruel pain or bad kill happening to comrades.'

CHAPTER 39

THEY HIT ALEXANDER WHERE IT HURTS

Alexander felt his bonds loosen.

What was that about his *comrades*? Maybe . . . Could it possibly . . . ? Hope leaped in his heart. He scoured the room, and noticed something he had missed before. As well as the Borgia actively swarming around him in the torture chamber, there were also Borgia hanging around the walls like shy kids at the school disco. They were, Alexander realized, more of the same storage drones in which he'd been transported.

And as he looked at the blobby brainless creatures, he saw that they weren't empty. He could see inside them the shapes of his friends. Make out faces, even expressions.

Their eyes were open. They were watching him, helpless. Jamie, Felicity, Melvyn, Really Annoying Girl, The Hurricane, Magic Titch, Tortoise Boy, and there, on his own, Cedric, as glum as ever.

Alexander was torn between the joy of seeing that his friends had not (yet) been eaten, and the horror of their plight.

Then he noticed something odd about the Borgia drone that encased Cedric. He didn't know much – well, anything – about Borgia physiology or anatomy, but he got the distinct feeling that this particular specimen wasn't well. Rather than the lurid green of the standard Borgia complexion, this fellow was a faint pink, with some splodges of brown. It reminded him vaguely of the rotten fruit you'd find on the street after the market traders had gone home. Alexander felt the underpants working again. They were trying to tell him something. Something important. But there was too much to take in, too many things happening, and Alexander's head began to throb with confusion.

More orders were vented by Thlugg. Some words leaked into the translator, but nothing that Alexander could make sense of. Then one of the drones began to wriggle. It was the one containing Really Annoying Girl, still clutching her lethal, bejewelled school bag. Alexander could see the panic on her face.

Actually, it wasn't panic. More like rage.

With a rippling convulsion the drone expelled her onto the floor, where she slid on her back for a couple of metres before coming to a stop.

'I knew you was gonna—' she said, or tried to say, but her mouth was full of slime, and it came out as a burbling babble. She was held fast by two Borgia guards, and a third oozed towards her.

Then the voice came again, and Alexander knew he was supposed to hear the order that followed.

'Human female eat. Do not kill yet. Make bad feeling of being eat last long time. Begin with pedal extremities. End with spongy grey organ of thinking with.'

Then the third Borgia guard began to engulf Really Annoying Girl from the shoes up. Alexander watched in horrified fascination as the powerful Borgia digestive juices began to dissolve her trainers. It was all visible through the semi-transparent jellied flesh.

Finally, Really Annoying Girl found her natural voice. 'Oi, them's new, you stupid lump of snot!'

Brave though Really Annoying Girl was, Alexander knew that soon the trainers would be gone and then the pain would start. And in fact that was already happening. The juices had worked their way in at the ankles, and Really Annoying Girl was starting to look uncomfortable (as well as annoyed).

'Enough!' he said. 'I'll talk.'

'Excellent very,' sighed Thlugg. 'Commence.'

Alexander did his best to sound as if he knew what he was talking about, clearing his mind to let the pants speak for him. He had to buy time. For what? He didn't know yet, but somehow he knew that Einstein's underpants would come to the rescue.

'The defence shield runs on the Linux operating system. The entry code is one-seven-six-eight-nine QQGY. You can access the system by sending a radio wave repeat-ing the musical notes G, A, F, F, C, where the second F is an octave lower than the first. This will deactivate the anti-virus and spy-ware module. The warheads are a neutrino-based zilium alloy. Converting their output to standard thermonuclear mega-tonnage isn't really appropriate, as they work more through molecular disrup-tion rather than simple blast or radiation damage. The secret of a good pizza is a thin base, but only if cooked in a wood-fired oven, giving good heat from all directions. Use a mixture of mozzarella and provolone cheese. A waiter with a really enormous pepper grinder will add greatly to the spectacle. Got that?'

There was a pause. Thlugg looked at his chief science officer, Colonel Paaarp. Paaarp, who was also the acting technical head of the Torture and Maiming Department (*acting* head because Thlugg had recently eaten the official head), shrugged a heavy Borgia shrug, and vented noncommittally:

'I suspect the Earthling is talking out of his rear venting hole. But it will not take us long to ascertain this.'

Before Thlugg had the chance to respond, a breathless Borgia female entered the chamber.

Thlugg looked at the attractive young thing, and drooled a little. He would, he decided, have her delivered to his quarters later on. Her behaviour would dictate whether the pleasures pandered to would be culinary or carnal.

'Lord, there is a . . . situation.'

'Situation? Speak plain, girl, or be humphlejabbed.'

'Sire, I think you should return to the command deck. An object has been detected—'

'Enough. I go. This had better be worth my time.'

Yes, thought Thlugg: *she will be humphlejabbed and* then *eaten*.

Before he left he returned his attention to Alexander.

'This given me information. If wrong, not change any. Still we crush your planet. But also extra will you suffer. We you make pain until your hurt capacity exhausted is. Amusing it will be to see how long that time length is. Skilled, we are, in making last. Live you may long enough to see your planet enslaved. You may enough not. In either case, when time comes we kill you. Slowly.

As leader, you will have privilege of watching the die others. First courses of our banquet you will see. Last course you will not see. The last course will be you. Ha ha ha.'

Then, with the other Borgia, he left, but not before issuing a final order.

'Vomit forth the worms,' he vented, in the direction of the brainless storage drones, as the heavy door slithered shut behind him. 'Apart let them tear themselves, before finish the job we will.'

Brutal monster Thlugg may have been, but his psychology was ever acute.

CHAPTER 40

THE RECKONING

'Are you OK?' Alexander asked.

Really Annoying Girl looked at him like he was mad. 'Yeah, course I'm OK, because, like, I've just been having a right good old time, haven't I? I just loves being eaten, puked up and then eaten again. Better than Disneyland, innit?'

Alexander was relieved that at least some of the old fire was back. But there were tears in her eyes. She was human, after all. He squeezed her hand.

'Gerroff!' she said, but when he began to pull his hand away she gripped it.

Together they watched in fascination as, one by one, the drones spewed out the other FREAKs. Alexander helped wipe the mucus out of their eyes, and clapped them on the back until they'd brought up the worst of the gunk.

In a few minutes they were reunited again.

'Thank God you're all fine,' Alexander said. 'When I first saw you inside those . . . those things, I thought . . .'

'I'm actually not sure that fine is what we are,' said Melvyn, and proved the point by spewing up a final squirt of goo.

Alexander looked at them again. Tortoise Boy, Melvyn, Felicity, Really Annoying Girl, Jamie, The Hurricane, Magic Titch. They were bleak and broken and spent. They looked like they'd been hollowed out. They were covered in mucus, drying now into crusty flakes. They looked like the lepers in his *Horrible History* book. He guessed he looked pretty terrible too.

'Don't feel good,' said Jamie. 'Didn't like being in that smelly belly. Had enough adventures. Want to go home now.'

'I know, Jamie. But you've been really brave.'

Alexander felt his throat catch. He'd led Jamie into this deadly peril. Led them all. And he didn't know how to lead him out again.

Then Titch said, 'What have you got on your head? It's not those—'

'Pants, yes. Einstein's underpants. They've been helping—'

But before he could go on, a groan came from Tortoise Boy.

'Cedric? Where's Cedric?'

Alexander remembered the sick-looking drone.

'Here, I think . . .'

They all gathered round. The drone had now lost its shape, and looked more like a puddle than a monstrous alien being. Its flesh had turned completely grey. Cedric stared out from the midst of it, unblinking.

'Do you think he's—' Melvyn began.

But Tortoise Boy shoved his hand straight into the mess and pulled out his beloved companion. 'Cedric, Cedric,' he implored. 'Speak to me!'

'Maybe he needs the kiss of life,' said Felicity.

Tortoise Boy didn't need a second invitation. He lowered his mouth towards the dry reptilian lips. But before he made contact Felicity cried out:

'Hey, he moved! He definitely moved!'

And, yes, the eyelids flickered, and Cedric's pink tongue came out for a wiggle.

Tortoise Boy drew back. 'Cedric, you're OK,' he sighed, and hugged the impassive tortoise to his chest.

'Well, that's sweet,' came the squeaky voice of Magic Titch, 'but it doesn't change the fact that we are up to our neck in *you know what*. And we all know whose fault it is – the Underpant Kid.'

'I knew you was gonna say that. And it's true,' added Really Annoying Girl as they all swivelled away from Cedric and stared at Alexander.

Alexander glared back at them. He

couldn't believe they still doubted him after everything that had happened.

'But don't you *see*? Otto was right about the invasion, about these pants, about *everything*. These monsters are trying to destroy the Earth and . . . and . . .'

'But what use are we?' said Felicity. 'It should be grown-ups doing this, not us. I'm frightened and I want to go home. We all do.'

The others shouted their agreement. Even Melvyn.

'But you *must* understand,' Alexander implored. 'We're the Earth's last hope.'

'You mean because of our special powers?' said Titch, with bitter sarcasm.

'Yeah, well—'

'Because, you see, I've been thinking about that. In fact I was doing a lot of thinking inside that thing' – he gestured with his thumb towards the drone that had puked him up – 'and I've got a good memory, me. You have to have a good memory when you're a magician. No good forgetting how to do a trick halfway through, is there?'

'What are you getting at, Titch?' said Melvyn.

But Alexander already had a sinking feeling in his stomach.

'I was doing some maths in my head. And I may not be as quick as the genius here, but I can do multiplication if I think about it hard enough, setting it all out like it's on paper. And I thought I'd do that to take my mind off where I was, and what was happening to me.'

'So what?' said Really Annoying Girl. ''Cos, like, this is really boring up to now, and I don't want to add being bored to all the other useless things going on.'

'It'll all become clear in just one minute. Remember you knew the square root of two hundred and eighty-nine?'

'Yes, well, it wasn't *that* hard, just—'

'No, not that hard. But the next one was – the square root of twenty-one thousand, eight hundred and seventy-four point four one, as I recall.'

'He got it right again, though, didn't he?' said Melvyn. 'We checked. It was amazing.'

'He did, and I can't explain it, except by luck – sheer, amazing fluke.'

'But what about the others? He got even harder ones right. And they can't *all* have been luck.'

'Ah, that's exactly my point. You see, that was the last one we actually checked on the calculator. But now I've checked in my head. And he got them all wrong.'

There was a gasp. And a tut (from Really Annoying Girl).

'No way you could remember.'

'I can, and I did. The first was: *What is the square root of one hundred and twenty-three million?* That's right, isn't it, TB? It was you that asked it.'

Tortoise Boy looked up from Cedric. 'Yeah, that's right. I think.'

'And you said—'

Alexander completed the sentence for him: 'Nineteen thousand four hundred and eighty.'

'Precisely. And even though I can't tell you what the square root of a hundred and twenty-three million is, I can tell you it's not nineteen thousand four hundred and eighty, because I did it my head, like I said, and nineteen thousand four hundred and eighty squared is three hundred and seventy-nine million, four hundred and seventy thousand, and four hundred exactly. And if you don't believe me, write it all down and do the sum yourselves.'

Titch said all this with his eyes burning into Alexander like lasers.

'And it's the same with all the others. *Wrong. Wrong. Wrong.* Those things on your head are just a pair of stinky old tramp's grundies. They've got about as much to do with Einstein as my mum's knickers have. Alexander is a fraud. A liar. And we're here for nothing.'

'Who are you to talk?' said Felicity, using

a voice that none of them had ever heard her use before. 'You're supposed to be a magician, but what have you ever done that's magic?'

And then it was a free-for-all, with accusations and recriminations buzzing like flies around fresh cow dung.

'. . . and I thought you were going to organize us. Well, you've organized us into getting mashed.'

'Well, at least you've lived up to your name, you annoying . . .'

'. . . tortoise! What's the blinking point of that?'

'. . . and you, you're just boring . . .'

'. . . boring's better than stinking . . .'

'. . . at least I'm not the eighth blinking dwarf . . .'

Then there was a brief pause as they all drew breath. Titch took the opportunity to focus his anger once again on Alexander.

'Everyone's right,' he said. 'Absolutely one hundred per cent right. We're just a bunch of losers. Freaks, in fact. But not like the flipping Fellowship of Really Awesome Kids. Just freaks, plain and simple. And now we're all going to die. Because. Of. You.'

Alexander looked from face to face. Titch was as hard as quartz. Really Annoying Girl viewed him with open hostility. Tortoise Boy and Cedric were both grim. Jamie looked lost. Melvyn stared at the dungeon floor, and Felicity looked like she'd been betrayed.

She was right. She *had* been betrayed. The FREAKs were a waste of time. The FREAKs were nothing. And he was the biggest nothing of all. Slowly, as they all watched, he began to remove Einstein's useless underpants from his head.

But before Alexander could finish the job, the door opened again, and so the erstwhile leader of the once glorious and noble FREAKs was left to confront the new challenge half in and half out of the scraggy old pants.

CHAPTER 41

A GLIMMER...

It was hard to be sure, but Alexander thought he recognized the small Borgia who came gliding into the torture chamber. The strange thing was that this Borgia was on its own. And unarmed. Both in the sense of having no arms and not having a weapon.

'Let's jump it,' hissed Tortoise Boy, determined to get revenge for the injuries done to Cedric.

'Yeah,' said Titch. 'Let's at least go down fighting.'

Alexander felt that this was a bad idea, but it was, surprisingly, The Hurricane who spoke up.

'Hold on, guys. I think... I think she comes in peace.'

'How the heck would you know she comes in peace?' said Titch.

'And how do you know she's a she?' added Felicity.

'I can sort of sense it . . . No, I can *smell* it.'

While they were debating, the Borgia slimed its way straight to the translation device, and began to waft gas with some urgency.

'Plymm my name is,' came the voice. It was subtly less mechanical than before, and carried an almost feminine tone. 'In your language means Smells of Wild Flowers. Time is not plenty. Quickly must be. I am navigation officer. We have found tiny planet coming. Tiny planet will hit Earth. Smash. All dead. Bad is this for Thlugg. Bad for Borgia. All smash, not any left to eat.'

'WHAT?' yelled the FREAKs in unison.

'Yes, tiny planet smash Earth.'

'This can't be . . .'

'No!'

'But . . . but . . .'

'I knew I was unlucky, but this is ridiculous.'

'Hang on,' said Alexander, who like the others was struggling to take in the true meaning of what the Borgia was saying. 'Is there nothing you can do? Do you have some sort of plan?'

'Plan? Yes, plan I have. Is small chance only. Thlugg pride much high. Will not want to lose meat on Earth or face with Borgia High Council. Will use ship's energy shield to try to deflect very small planet away from Earth. This dangerous is. Might not work. If not work then ship go bang. No more Thlugg. No more Borgia invasion.'

Plymm – who, as you've probably worked out, was that same pretty little Borgia female slavered over by Thlugg – paused, and Alexander cut in:

'I don't . . . I don't understand. Why are you telling us this? Why do you want to help us? We're human, you're an . . . an . . . alien . . .'

After a gap for the words to be translated into smells, Plymm answered: 'Thlugg eat Vice-Admiral Jlatt. Jlatt my . . . what you call by name boyfriend. I hate now. Want to harm. Also I believe Borgia must find new way to live, not always kill kill eat eat. Other like me on home planet. Help our cause if no more warmonger like Thlugg. Also cute I think humans. Like furry top area to stroke . . .'

Then Plymm stretched out a sinuous, protoplasmic arm towards The Hurricane. As it travelled, it became more human-like, growing long fingers. These long fingers then caressed and ruffled The Hurricane's greasy hair, making him blush so deeply that his zits were briefly camouflaged.

'Get a room,' said Really Annoying Girl.

Alexander felt an irrational spurt of hope. Was there really a chance? A chance for them, a chance for humanity?

Almost without thinking, he pulled Einstein's pants down over his ears.

'So what do we do?' he said. 'Just wait here to see what happens?'

'No. Must help to make Thlugg fail. We destroy energy shield generators. Wait till last small time before bang. Then Thlugg nothing he can do. Then Thlugg die.'

'How do we know we can trust you?'

'Alternative yours is?'

There was a silence. Of course none of them had an alternative. Their backs were against the wall. A wall made of deadly spikes. With poisoned tips. And dynamite.

'Have I got this straight?' said Titch. 'If this plan works, then we get blown to bits along with these monsters. And if it fails, we get eaten?'

'Big pain first. Then eaten,' corrected Plymm.

'Great.'

'But if it works, at least our families and all the other people will be safe,' said Felicity.

'Is other small chance,' said Plymm. 'After

disable energy shield, we make move fast to escape pods. Probably not make it, but little chance worth big try.'

'Good enough for me,' said Alexander. 'What do you think, Jamie?'

Jamie nodded. 'We get 'em.'

'Right, that's it then. A chance is a chance, no matter how slim.'

CHAPTER 42

TOOLING UP

'Excuse me,' said Titch. 'In case you've forgotten, you're not our leader any more. We've already worked out that you are a fraud and a liar. So you don't get to decide what we do or don't do.'

'Just a second, Titch,' said Tortoise Boy. 'This sounds like a chance to get back at these creeps. Unless, like that girl monster says, you've got a better idea . . . ?'

'Well, er, no. And I'm not saying that we shouldn't do it, just that it's not up to this doofus and his crazy underpants.'

'Well, let's vote, then,' said Felicity. 'All in favour say yes.'

Everyone said yes except for Really Annoying Girl, who said, 'I knew you was gonna say that.' But then even she said yes as well.

'Good, it's decided,' said Alexander. 'One more thing though, Plymm: how are we going to make it to the shield generators? This ship is swarming with Borgia.'

'We fight.'

'But how? We don't have any weapons . . .' said Felicity.

'You have these,' said Plymm, and regurgitated the toy ray guns that Jamie, Alexander and The Hurricane had used before. 'I have modified them so that their output is more deadly for Borgia. But rubbish Earth batteries nearly extinguish and Borgia do not use AA battery size, but AAAs. So must use carefully. Two, maybe three shots each.'

'That'll never be enough,' said Melvyn.

'I've got another idea,' said Alexander.

'It's your ideas that got us here in the first place,' said Titch.

'Let's hear it anyway,' said Felicity.

'Thanks. We've all seen what happened to that Borgia drone that had Cedric inside it.'

'Yeah,' said Jamie. 'Melted all yucky. Like when I kept a sausage under my bed for a midnight feast, then forgot till next year.'

'Exactly, Jamie. That can only mean one thing — tortoises are poisonous to the Borgia. And the drones have a greatly reduced metabolism, so we can expect the tortoise toxin to act much more quickly on the proper Borgia.'

Metabolism? Alexander didn't realize he even knew that word. The pants were really on fire.

Tortoise Boy began to grin. 'So what do I do? Just sort of smash them with Cedric?'

'That's it. If you can break through the outer coating and get Cedric to the pulp, you'll disable them straight away.'

'Why don't we test it on this one?' said Titch.

'No,' said Alexander. 'We're allies, and the

FREAKs know how to stick by their friends.'

'Still,' said Melvyn thoughtfully, 'a couple of one-shot guns, plus TB whacking these things with Cedric . . . well, it's not very much to put up against the mightiest and evilest beings in the galaxy, is it?'

'You're right, Mel. But it's not all we've got—'

'If this is going to be some speech about having each other, and that making us invincible, then I'm going to be sick,' said Titch. 'Because it hasn't exactly worked so far, has it?'

'Well,' said Alexander, 'we *do* have each other, and together we *are* invincible. But I know something that makes us, er, invincibler.'

'What?' said several intrigued voices.

'Before you lot got puked, they tortured me using smells—'

'Gross,' said Really Annoying Girl.

'Yes, it was. But I learned something. The Borgia can't take a certain smell – I was listening to the translations that came through that machine when they were talking to each other.'

'What was the smell?' asked The Hurricane, suddenly very interested.

Alexander looked him in the eye. 'Eggy fart, hint of cabbage.'

The Hurricane smiled. 'I can manage that.'

'And I've got this,' said Really Annoying Girl, holding up her heavy-duty bag with its deadly jewel encrustations. 'Them fings is gonna pay for messin' wiv my shoes.'

And then, unexpectedly, Titch added: 'And I've got these.'

He pulled the set of lethal steel playing cards out of his sleeve.

Alexander looked thoughtfully at the glinting cards. 'I don't think they'll have much impact on their own . . .'

Then, once again, he felt the tingle from the pants. He had a vision. No longer was he in the bowels of the Borgia flagship –

now he was deep in the Amazonian rainforest. Indian hunters were gathered round a fire. One of them held a tiny, vividly coloured tree frog. His strong fingers gently squeezed the frog. A milky substance oozed from pores in its skin. The other hunters dipped the tips of their blow-pipe darts in the liquid.

Alexander snapped out of his trance. 'We need to get some, erm, juice out of Cedric,' he exclaimed. 'Then you can dip your darts – I mean, cards in it, Titch.'

'What, you want to squeeze him out like a lemon?' said Tortoise Boy, backing away. 'No one's getting any juice out of my Cedric!'

'Yuck!' said Really Annoying Girl. 'He's pooped on you.'

Cedric had left a dollop of green-brown poo on Tortoise Boy's trousers. The timing was perfect.

'That's it – exactly what we need. Titch, smear some of that stuff on your cards.'

'Gross. Must I?'

'You've seen what tortoise venom does to those things. It'll turn your cards into lethal poison darts.'

'Well, put that way . . . Maybe those pants are working after all. I don't think you could have come up with an idea like that without them.'

A minute later and they were ready to go.

Alexander took one of the ray guns for himself, and gave the other two to Melvyn and Felicity. It meant that each of them had something to fight with, except for Jamie. But then Jamie had his superstrength, and he no more needed weapons than did the Incredible Hulk.

Alexander was proud of them all.

'OK, Plymm,' he said, turning to their Borgia ally. 'Lead on.'

CHAPTER 43

THE BATTLE FOR THE FUTURE OF HUMANITY

Plymm vented into a control panel, and the door opened. The FREAKs spilled out into the corridor. As they emerged, two hulking Borgia sentinels glooped towards them from either side, thinking it was their lucky day: a chance to dine on some tasty humans with the excuse that they were just trying to prevent an escape.

'*Now!*' yelled Alexander, and Tortoise Boy, Really Annoying Girl and The Hurricane went to work.

Tortoise Boy rent the air with a piercing scream, and smashed Cedric down onto what would have been the first Borgia's skull, if the Borgia had bones. (Cedric, seeing what was coming, had retreated safely inside his shell.) The blow broke through the skin of the sentinel, causing instant paralysis and rapid liquefaction. Within seconds, the creature was reduced to a spreading puddle of gunk.

While that was happening, there was more action on the other side. First Really Annoying Girl gave a vicious right and left swipe combination, then it was The Hurricane's turn. This was no time for fancy manoeuvres, no time for showboating. The Hurricane just did a basic half-turn-and-leg-raise – the sort of move they'd teach you on your very first day at farting school, if there were such a thing – and then blasted the advancing Borgia with a sound like a moose coughing.

The effect was immediate, and most gratifying. The creature fell to the floor and writhed around like a breakdancing bogey. It foamed and frothed, and emitted gusts of yellow gas that even the humans could sense as cries of anguish and terror.

Luckily The Hurricane had directed almost all the fart's energy forwards, but, even so, there was inevitably some blowback. There was just a hint of the sort of smell you'd get when walking past a mad old lady's bungalow on a hot day. It didn't bother the FREAKs, but it was enough to send Plymm reeling back against the softly undulating wall.

It was then that Alexander noticed something odd about the alien. She was definitely less blobby than she had been when he first saw her. There were distinct indentations and subtle curves. The long arm she had stretched out to The Hurricane hadn't retracted fully into her body, and it was balanced by another, budding from her left side. There even seemed to be a groove forming down her lower half, as if legs were gradually beginning to separate.

But there was no time now to speculate about this latest curious development.

Alexander held out a hand to steady the

alien. Her flesh felt almost pleasant to the touch; not clammy and cold like the other Borgia, but cool and dry.

'Which way?' he said. And then he realized something. Without the translation device, they could not communicate.

'Let me try,' said The Hurricane. 'I think – and I know this sounds crazy – I think I can understand her. And speak a little of their language.'

'How the . . . ?'

'I don't know. I must have picked it up . . . something to do with my special ability.'

'Fine, well, ask her to lead the way.'

The Hurricane delicately burped at Plymm. Plymm shuddered with delight, and vented back. The Hurricane sniffed the air and smiled a little half-smile. Then Plymm began to glide down the corridor, wiggling her newly moulded hips as she went.

'Game on,' said The Hurricane.

'I knew you was gonna say that,' said

Really Annoying Girl, but in a less strident voice than usual.

As Alexander was stepping over the body of the fart-blasted Borgia, he saw it twitch. He thought it was going to make a grab for him and he automatically shrank away. But the Borgia wasn't after him. It squirted a weak stream of gas towards a control panel. Instantly the whole corridor began to throb, and the Borgia alarm smell filled the space. It was the smell of a cat thrown onto a fire.

'*Move, move, move!*' yelled Alexander, and they sped down the corridor.

It wasn't long before they hit more trouble. A squad of Borgia troopers were waiting round one of the bends. They were armed with plasma cannon, and shots ricocheted off the walls and ceiling.

Alexander looked expectantly at The Hurricane.

He shook his head. 'Out of range. And they'll fry me before I get close enough.'

'TB won't make it either,' said Alexander. 'We'll just have to use the ray guns.'

'Don't forget me and these babies,' said Titch, holding up his Death Cards.

Alexander smiled at him, and they held each other's gaze for a couple of seconds. Their argument was over. They were a team. They were the FREAKs.

'OK, guys, get ready. Select your targets carefully. And remember, the guns are only going to stun them. We'll have to go in and finish the job by hand. Right – one, two, three—'

But the eager FREAKs couldn't wait, and the 'three' was drowned out by the cacophonous blaring of the toy guns. More silent, but also more deadly, were the razor-sharp, poisoned Death Cards, which flew like hell's frisbees to their targets.

'They're down!' yelled Tortoise Boy, already charging towards the creatures. He was closely followed by Jamie and Really Annoying Girl.

'*AAAAAAARRRRRRGGGGGGHH-HHHHH!*' screamed Tortoise Boy.

'*SSSSUUUUUPPPPEEERRRRSSSS-TTTTTRRRRROONNNNGGGGG!*' bellowed Jamie.

'I KNEW YOU WAS GONNA SAY THAT,' yelled Really Annoying Girl, although no one knew who on earth she was talking to.

Together they tore into the already crippled Borgia. Cedric pulped them, Jamie walloped them, Really Annoying Girl whacked them, and by the time the others arrived, the Borgia were just stains.

Plymm vented gas. It smelled minty, with undertones of leaf mould and Chinese takeaway. The Hurricane sniffed, and translated.

'The shield generators are this way.'

CHAPTER 44

AND ADMIRAL THLUGG...?

Back on the command deck, Admiral Thlugg had other things on his mind. Well, one rather big thing, actually.

The approach of Asteroid c4098 was most inconvenient. He knew what his enemies and political opponents back on the home-world would say. They'd whisper that he had been negligent. That he should have known of this wandering celestial body and inter-cepted it long before. They would say that he had lost a great harvest of delicious snacks.

And of course it would all be a gift to those pesky pinko vegetarian types, who would, if they got their way, have the fearsome Borgia warriors live on a diet of algae and roots.

Well, he would show them, show them

all, that there was life in old Thlugg yet.

Which was why he was about to play a game of space hockey, with the asteroid as the puck and his own flagship as the stick.

Risky.

But then the great Borgia Empire had been forged through risk-taking.

It required his full attention. When the news reached him that the prisoners had escaped, he literally bit the head (or rather dorsal half) off the unfortunate Borgia who had brought it. He then issued an order for the fugitives' recapture, with the strict instruction that he wanted to hear nothing further about this until the ship's tricky manoeuvre was completed.

He had to align his vessel at a precise angle to the oncoming asteroid. Get the angle wrong and he'd lose the ship as well as the Earth, with all its succulent goodness.

So even as fine a mind as Thlugg's, backed up by the most powerful computers in the universe, found itself fully occupied, for now.

CHAPTER 45

A CHEMISTRY LESSON

The FREAKs were lurking near the main entrance to the shield generator room. There were twenty burly, heavily armed Borgia on guard. Toy guns and metal playing cards and fierce tortoises wouldn't do the job. There was no way through.

The Hurricane was translating Plymm's smells in hushed tones: 'She says there's a ventilation shaft that will take us right inside the room. We can give the shield generators a serious mashing from there. Then we make a dash for the escape pods, and pray this all works.'

The opening to the ventilation shaft was a rubbery flap, like something you'd find in a dissected pig's heart. It was just wide enough for them to squeeze through. Then they had to wriggle like worms along the glistening intestinal tubing. It really wasn't at all nice in there. The foulest of foul gases wafted over them as they crawled, adding to that feeling that they were in the lower reaches of some great beast's bowels.

Alexander was in the middle of the crawling line of kids, his view restricted to Felicity's bottom. Not that he was looking. Jamie, Titch, Melvyn and Really Annoying Girl jostled behind him, while Tortoise Boy, The Hurricane and Plymm were ahead of Felicity. The thinking was to get their heavy hitters – Tortoise Boy and The Hurricane – up at the front for when they dropped down into the shield generator room.

Suddenly Alexander became aware of a commotion from the back of the line.

'Monsters coming!' Jamie yelled, panic in his voice.

'Attacked from the rear – sneaky alien swine!' snarled Titch.

'I knew you was gonna snarl that,' said Really Annoying Girl.

'Slow them down, Titch,' Alexander cried, looking back over his shoulder. 'What have you got?'

'All out of Death Cards. Nothing else, just rubbish: a rubber chicken, fake rabbit . . . No, wait, there's the flash-bombs I use when I want to disappear. You know — big flash, lots of smoke, and I go hide. That might confuse them for a while.'

Alexander now saw the first of the pursuing Borgia. It was moving swiftly through the narrow passage, squirming along like a finger in a nostril.

'Do it.'

Titch dug around in his pocket and found three of the flash-bombs — tiny parcels of gunpowder, designed to go off with a bang on contact. He hurled them back along the tunnel, shouting out, '*SHAZAM!*' as he did so.

What happened next was surprising to

anyone who did not know that the venting gases of the Borgia were about seventy per cent methane, with smaller amounts of hydrogen, hydrogen sulphide and carbon monoxide.

What happened was:

BOOM!

Alexander was suddenly granted a profound insight into what it must feel like to be a cannonball, as the detonation sent the FREAKs flying along the few remaining metres of tubing and out onto the floor of the shield power-generating facility.

CHAPTER 46
THE GREAT DILEMMA

The ventilation shaft entered the shield room at floor level, which meant that they came skidding out on their bums, rather than crash-landing on their heads.

Their sudden and dramatic appearance was as startling to the half-dozen Borgia technicians as it was to the FREAKs. This was a further piece of luck, as, with ringing ears, hazy vision and wobbly legs, they were in no condition to fight straight away.

Really Annoying Girl was the first to recover. Years of having to listen to her own raucous voice had left her immune to loud, unpleasant noises. She went to work with her bag, flailing right and left like a berserker Viking warrior. The technicians were not battle-trained, and two fell before her onslaught like corn before the scythe.

Tortoise Boy was next onto his feet, and soon he and Cedric had taken out two more, the unfortunate creatures left liquefying on the floor.

The last two made a wobbling run for the door. The Hurricane gassed one with a quick spurt of eggy cabbage (or cabbagy egg), and Jamie clutched the second in his mighty embrace. But it was like trying to grab the soap in the bath, and it squirted free. It hit the control panel and sped through the opening door, venting a warning to the guards as it went.

Plymm was at the door a second later. She had the override code, and locked it down.

Well, it was Plymm and yet not Plymm. She now looked more like a human than a Borgia blob.

She sent out a gaseous message to The Hurricane.

'She says that will hold them for a few minutes.'

'Could you ask her why she suddenly looks like a . . . like a *girl*,' said Alexander.

There was a quick exchange of smells.

'She says that when they are young, the Borgia are more, um, malleable. If that's the word. They can change shape. They lose that ability as they reach adulthood. She likes the way we look, so she's adopting our form. But it means she'll be like this for ever.'

As The Hurricane spoke, Plymm moved around the room, smashing dials, throwing switches, wrenching out wiring. The others joined in, performing more or less random acts of vandalism. It may not have contributed much to disabling the shield, but it certainly made them feel better.

As they worked, they heard the hissing sound of a laser torch cutting through the door. And then a louder humming sound filled the ship, followed by an ominous silence.

'That's it,' said Plymm, through The Hurricane.

Actually, not just through The Hurricane. For the first time, her venting was accompanied by a barely audible, inarticulate, but still recognizable version of the words.

The Borgia was learning to speak. The FREAKs were too busy to be freaked by this.

'Now we go,' she whispered ploppily. 'We have seven minutes. We go escape pod through breathing tube how we came.'

They began to crowd around the ventilation shaft, desperate to grasp this one slim chance of life.

'Wait,' said Melvyn.

'No,' stressed The Hurricane. 'You heard her: we've got to get out of here!'

Alexander began to say something, but Melvyn stopped him.

'This is important. I've thought it through. Plymm says that this will work if we're lucky. Put that the other way round. It will work if the Borgia and that monster, Thlugg, are *unlucky*. It means that we're relying on chance, on fortune. And this is too important for that. Well, I know how to change the odds.'

'What are you on about?' said Titch.

'Guys, we got to split,' added The Hurricane. 'Like, now.'

Alexander was ahead of the others. Melvyn was his best friend, and he knew what he was thinking.

'Mel, no—'

Melvyn put his hand up. 'Enough, Alexander. I'm staying on this ship, and that's that. If I stay, the asteroid will smash it to pieces. If I go, it won't. It's a luck thing. I'm going to keep my bad luck here with me where it can do some good. It's why I'm here. It's my power.'

'Well,' said Really Annoying Girl, 'I did *not* know you was gonna say that.'

'I can stay right here with the remaining

ray guns and take out any blob that tries to get through that door.'

Alexander looked at the door. The Borgia were nearly through.

'You know this is the right thing, Alexander,' Melvyn continued. 'You want to be a leader? Well, now's the time to lead. Get them out of here.'

Plymm had been following the conversation, helped by The Hurricane. She touched Alexander gently on the arm. 'Boy right,' she whispered. 'He stay here and stop Borgia come fix shield. But now we go or all die.'

Alexander looked around at the others. Felicity was crying. Heck, they were all crying.

'Jamie stay too. Help my friend.'

'If he stays, I stay,' said Tortoise Boy.

'And me,' said Titch.

That was it. Alexander had to act to save them, even if it meant sacrificing his best friend.

'No, Melvyn's right. Let's go,' he said,

desperately trying hide his own emotion.

Felicity let out a wail of despair, but Alexander grabbed her roughly, and dragged her towards the ventilation shaft.

'Please, Felicity, do this for me. I have to save you. I have to . . . Think about Jamie – we can't let him die here.'

Felicity nodded, and with tears streaming down her face, she took Jamie by the hand and led him into the shaft.

The Hurricane and Plymm helped shepherd the others after them. Alexander was the last to enter.

'Get going,' he screamed. 'I'll see you there.'

CHAPTER 47

BUTCH AND SUNDANCE

Then, as quietly as he could, he crawled back out again. Melvyn was waiting by the door, a ray gun in each hand.

'I'll take one of those,' Alexander said to his startled friend.

'But . . . no . . . you've got to go!'

Einstein's underpants had become rather skewed. Alexander tugged them determinedly down over his ears. 'I'm seeing this through with you.'

'But it's *my* luck, *my* rotten luck, not yours.'

'Mel, I've been with you every time you've had a bucket of paint dropped on your head; every time you've fallen into a manhole; every time you've almost been killed by an out-of-control ice-cream van; every time you've been bashed and bumped and scraped. And I'm going to stay with you now.'

Melvyn started to reply, but even though these were going to be his best friend's last words, Alexander found himself zoning out.

He was having an idea.

An amazing idea.

He tingled with the electric fizz of genius.

Actually, *idea* wasn't quite the right word. He was experiencing *understanding*. Things that had been clouded were now becoming clear.

'What are you smiling about?' said Melvyn, puzzled.

But Alexander just grabbed his arm and, laughing now, said, 'There's no need . . . We have to get off . . . The . . . It's . . . I'll explain on the way.'

Melvyn could not resist him. Together they dived into the shaft and scuttled after the others. Along the way the path subdivided many times, but they were able to follow the scent trail left by The Hurricane and Plymm's conversations. And soon they saw a dark shape ahead of them.

'Hey,' yelled Alexander, 'we're coming!'

Seconds later they were all dropping out into a new compartment. It was a wide circular space, and the walls were lined with escape pods, each with enough room for all the children and Plymm.

The others crowded round Alexander and Melvyn, their expressions perplexed, puzzled, joyous.

'I worked it out,' gasped Alexander. 'Melvyn's not *unlucky* at all. In fact he's amazingly *lucky*. All those terrible accidents, and he's never once got seriously hurt. What's the chance of that? Anyone normal who fell out of a window or tripped over an eyelash or whatever would have ended up in hospital. But not Melvyn. He's not *Unluckeon*, he's *Luckeon*!'

And Melvyn smiled a slow smile of recognition. 'Luckeon,' he said. 'I like it.'

And then Plymm urged them into one of the pods, using what were now long, elegant arms and delicate fingers. As they strapped themselves in (loosely, for of course the seats were designed for Borgia proportions), she rapidly pressed a sequence into the control panel buttons. A handle eased down from the cockpit roof, and she yanked it.

The pod whooshed down a launching tube and out into the vacuum of space.

CHAPTER 48
DOWN THE THLUGG-HOLE

'Shield!' screamed the admiral. 'Where is that shield? GET ME MY SHIELD!'

'It . . . appears . . . to be—' But those were the last smells ever emitted by that particular Borgia officer, as he was split and sucked dry by Thlugg, the way an ape eats an orange.

'Fools!' Thlugg splurted. 'Side thrusters, full impulse power. And get me a visual on that thing.'

A glowing green representation of Asteroid c4098 was projected in 3D glory into the middle of the command deck. It grew by the second, until its dimensions were greater than the room, and they were all contained within it.

'Why aren't we moving? Where are those thrusters? Who . . . ? What . . . ? Why . . . ?'

And then Thlugg began to laugh.

He laughed because the Borgia, although nasty, brutal, smelly and silly, are not cowards, and every Borgia likes to meet his fate laughing.

The explosion was the single brightest event in the history of the Earth. Where it had been night, it was day. Where it was day, the Sun suddenly appeared like a smudge of dark brown against the new light's intensity.

If the FREAKs had been looking back, they would have been blinded. But their eyes were on the blue Earth as it sped towards them.

'Whoooaahh!' they said, in one voice.

And, with the brightness filling the frail vessel, Alexander looked around at his companions, gazing into the eyes of each one.

There was Titch, whose poisoned Death Cards had cut a swathe through their foes, whose flashes had baffled their pursuers and propelled them magically to their destination.

There was Tortoise Boy, Cedric snoozing on his lap. Without them, they would never have battered their way through the Borgia guards.

There was The Hurricane, hand in hand with the lovely green Plymm. Where would they have been without his bottom? Without her help?

There was Really Annoying Girl, still clutching her lethal handbag, her face almost beautiful now that it was in repose.

And there was Jamie Superstrong, asleep and smiling in his sleep, because his mind was as pure as his body was strong, and he could sleep whenever he closed his eyes, and his dreams were always happy dreams.

And Felicity, who made him blush now by gazing back at him. Had he perhaps done it all for her?

And last, Unluckeon, now reborn as

Luckeon. Melvyn, his bestest friend in the whole wide world, who had been prepared to sacrifice himself to save them all.

No, not last, because there, reflected in the thick glass of the escape pod's window, was his own face. The face not of a genius, but of an ordinary boy who had saved the planet.

EPILOGUE
OTTO, AGAIN

'And the escape pod brought you back to England? That was nice. Could have been Siberia. Or Belgium.'

Uncle Otto had a room all to himself at the psychiatric hospital, but he liked to potter about in the grounds when the weather was sunny. He was now sitting on a bench under an enormous beech tree, with a tartan rug over his knees. The hospital staff were kind and let him wear his tin-foil helmet under a woolly hat, to prevent mind-reading. He was surrounded by photos and articles he'd cut out of magazines.

'That was Plymm. She's a pretty nifty space pilot.'

Uncle Otto nodded. 'And now she's

taken fully human form?'

'Yeah. She's still a bit, you know, *green*. But she's kind of foxy. For an alien. She goes to our school now. Lives in The Hurricane's spare room. I think they have a thing going on, which is kind of weird. But at least he's got a girlfriend at last.'

'And brilliant, the way you worked out that your friend Melvyn was really lucky after all. It was just the twist the story needed.'

'I'd never have done it without Einstein's underpants.'

'Ah, the pants,' said Otto craftily. 'You'll have finished with them then . . . ?'

'Oh . . . well, I was kind of hoping . . .'

Otto's eyes suddenly blazed red. 'They are my . . . *precious*.'

'Precious?' Alexander edged away a little. 'But they're only . . . and I was sort of hoping I could keep them — you know, for the next time we need to save the world.'

Otto passed his hand over his face, and

then seemed to recover himself. 'And they call *me* crazy. It wasn't the pants. It was you. You're the genius. The pants were just . . . well, they were scaffolding. And when the building's finished, you take the scaffolding away.'

Alexander nodded. 'I'll bring them next time I come.'

'Oh, I'll be out of here soon. You can drop them off to me at home. I'm a bit short on pants. I don't like the modern ones. They have electronic tags so the authorities know where you are.'

Alexander looked at Otto. Was he mad? Was he joking? It was hard to tell.

Then a nurse appeared beside them under the tree. 'I think that's enough for today,' she said, smiling at Alexander. And then, to Otto, 'And time for your meds, Mr Richards. Let's go in.'

Alexander said goodbye to Otto. As they shook hands, Otto said, 'You did well, boy. You did very well.'

'Thanks, Uncle.'

As Alexander walked away, he found that he was rather uncomfortable. He paused, shook one leg, wriggled around and dug his fingers into his pockets, trying not to draw too much attention to himself.

Einstein's underpants may have helped to save the world, but they didn't half ride up.

ACKNOWLEDGEMENTS

I'd like to thank Kelly Hurst, Alex Antscherl and Sophie Nelson for their efforts to turn a flabby mess into a lean, mean fightin' machine. But most of all I'd like to thank the wondrous Philippa Milnes-Smith for bending it, and me, into shape.